From an early age, Jim has had a love of writing and telling stories. When he was in his twenties he began sending articles into magazines and local newspapers. They were usually short stories. One of these stories, *Lost Love*, was adapted into a film by an independent filmmaker in the UK. The film was called *The Other Side of the Lake* and went on to win awards at film festivals. Jim played a part in the film. In 2020 he had a book published in the UK called *The Sad Windows*. Since *The Sad Windows*, Jim has been writing his latest novel, *No Light in his Eyes*. Like the first book, it deals with the what if's in life along with a supernatural theme. He enjoys writing, history, and walking in his spare time. Jim lives in Dublin with his wife and family.

For Dad and all the great times we had together.

Jim Burke

NO LIGHT IN HIS EYES

AUSTIN MACAULEY PUBLISHERS™

LONDON · CAMBRIDGE · NEW YORK · SHARJAH

A CIP catalogue record for this title is available from the British Library.

ISBN 9781398478046 (Paperback)
ISBN 9781398478053 (ePub e-book)

www.austinmacauley.com

First Published 2022
Austin Macauley Publishers Ltd®
1 Canada Square
Canary Wharf
London
E14 5AA

Acknowledgements

Thank you to my family for all their support.

Prologue

Around him everything was quiet. Now and again, he heard the sound of a bird making a screeching noise in the black night sky. All was still and peaceful except in John's head. He was young, frightened and forevermore uncertain of himself and those around him.

Chapter 1

John Hughes lay close to death on the narrow hospital bed. His heartbroken parents, brothers and sisters were gathered around him. They had been called in to say a final goodbye to their son and brother. They hadn't seen much of him in recent years. His unpleasant behaviour had succeeded in driving them away, and he had become hard and unfeeling. He hadn't always been that way, and his family often wondered what triggered the change in him. He knew he was dying, but he wasn't frightened. No, fear of death was not a concern for him. It was the feelings of sadness and regret that he found so hard to bear. He now felt sorry about the way he'd lived his life. He knew his family would of course be upset to have to let him go, but he also felt it would be a relief for them to be rid of him. They didn't feel that way, but he had become bitter and discontented, and that was the way he saw everything. It wasn't really the major cause of his sorrow though. He hadn't spent much time with them in recent years and reckoned they would forget him soon enough. His true misery in dying was due to the fact that he'd never found true love and experienced that wonderful feeling. He did love his family, but there wasn't that somebody special at his deathbed. They took turns at holding his limp white hand and patted it from time to time. Sometimes they whispered kind words in his ear, and though meant well, only served to make him feel a pitied wretch. He was rapidly growing weaker and could now barely sense them around his bed. He got some comfort from them being there, but he knew it was a lonely journey he would have to make. He had an awareness of his life fading away, and how close he was to the end. The feeling of sorrow and not being able to do anything was too much, and he now longed to leave the world behind him. His glazed eyes were reduced to tiny narrow slits and caused him to have a mean expression. He spotted a small patch of sunshine in the right-hand corner of the ceiling at the foot of his bed and tried with great difficulty to focus on it.

Suddenly, he noticed everything growing dimmer. The voices seemed to be getting further away and harder to hear. They sounded muffled, distorted and he could no longer make out what was being said. He felt his heartbeat slowing down like the chimes of a clock when it needed winding. This was followed quickly by a swishing sound in his ear and complete darkness. It lasted only for a second.

He now found himself standing in a long narrow room with a high ornate ceiling and pink walls. It was filled with a cool white swirling mist making his face feel moist and fresh. The hospital and his family had vanished. Through the mist, he could make out the shape of a man standing at the other end of the room. John watched as the figure came forward. He looked very old when he emerged fully from the mist, yet there was something youthful and fresh about him. He glowed with expectation and excitement. John had often noticed in life how this look usually vanished from people when they got to a certain age. The stranger still had it though, as well as having long white straight hair and an equally long white beard. He was wearing a deep brown linen coat with silver buttons all the way down to his feet and on the cuffs. The mist cleared, and the man with the beard pointed in the direction of two red cushioned armchairs. They looked incredibly old.

"You sit in that one, John, if you please."

"How do you know my name?" asked John sitting down and looking amazed. The old man stroked his beard and smiled.

"I know a lot of things about you. Do you know where you are or what's happened?"

"Am I dead?" asked John, dreading the reply.

"Yes, you are quite dead. What I mean to say is that you are dead in body. It is your soul, spirit, personality or whatever you want to call it that I am addressing now." John felt a strong urge to cry for his family and for himself. Moments before, he had wanted to die and now that he was dead, he felt sorry about everything. It seemed his chance of making any change in his life was now definitely gone forever. He wondered what heaven would hold in store for him. He'd only ever heard good things about it, and that to dwell there would be a far happier experience than being on earth.

"I can see into your mind, John. Yes, it is a happier place, and by now your soul would be passing through the different stages on its way if it was normal circumstances." John started to feel a horrible feeling of panic coming over him.

"Please don't tell me I'm going somewhere else. I know I've done things in life that I shouldn't have, but I never did anything terrible." The stranger raised his hand and motioned for John to stop. They sat looking each other in the eye, and the bearded man slowly put his finger to his lips. He then took it away and spoke in a hushed voice.

"I want you to be quiet now and listen carefully to me. When I want you to speak, I will tell you, do you understand?"

"Yes," said John, obediently, "you seem a bit cross for an angel. I'm presuming you are one."

"Well, it depends on who I'm talking to whether I need to be cross or not. Your behaviour in life after a certain point led to people avoiding you. You caused misery and heartache for a lot of people with your words and actions. You said mean things and made unnecessary trouble for them. You might think that this carry on wasn't terrible, but it was done with the intention of hurting. In this, you were successful and made unhappiness for many. Don't look shocked as if you don't know what I'm talking about." John's colour changed to red.

"Let us proceed now we've got that out of the way," said the old man, as if he wanted to hurry things along. "Allow me to introduce myself. My name is Rainbow, and yes, I am an angel." John tried to say something, but Rainbow put his finger to his lips again. John was silent. "It's not all about what one did in life," continued the angel, "but rather what one didn't that matters the most. We here in this place know all about your disappointment at not getting the chance to experience real love. Now you are dead, and the opportunity is taken away." John felt his eyes filling up and he cleared his throat of the choking lump he now felt there.

"You," said the angel, "did have a love early in life. Have you forgotten? Come now you must remember. You both could have continued together and brought it to the next stage. It was developing nicely, but through your own caution, confusion or circumstances let it fall by the wayside just as it was getting stronger. It was a terrible blunder. You know who I'm talking about, do you not?"

"Yes," answered John feeling ashamed and full of regret, "Clara. Maybe it wasn't entirely our fault, but yes I admit it could have been handled better."

"Why did you let her go? Maybe you know the answer. It's an important question. It could have been so different for both of you. You know something of her later life, but not all."

"Where is she now?" asked John.

"She's here in the spirit world and has been for a long time. She married, but life was not easy towards the end. Her husband was not well-chosen, and after a short illness, she died. She was very young."

"Oh, Clara. If she's here, can I see her?" The angel stroked his long beard again.

"No, not just at this time, but I have been instructed by a higher power than me to prepare you."

"What do you mean?" asked John, feeling mystified. Rainbow didn't speak for a moment, and he sat back with his long thin hands intertwined across his chest.

"There has been a meeting," he began, "it was about you. It was felt you were a soul who should have experienced what love really is. There are many souls here who have never found their soulmate, but it was decided by the great powers to take a closer look at your case. You're probably wondering what this is all about. We have observed you in life, and how your hardness at various times alienated people and cost you friends. It cost you love too, that special love you thought about as you lay dying in that hospital room. We know it was a mistake for you and Clara to part ways, and we know what you did since and how both your lives continued afterwards. Your trouble started not too long after you met her, imagine, that early on. So here you are at forty-five and dead from the result of a damaged heart. I'm not surprised it was your heart that killed you; it fits in with your lack of loving and being loved. Your soul suffers too when your heart suffers from unhappiness. Did you know that, John? For the last good number of years, it could be said that you were without both. Sound's harsh, doesn't it, but it's true, you were cold and lacked empathy, why?" John didn't answer and sat staring at his hands which were now beginning to tremble.

"You look very remorseful John but let me be clear with you. The supreme board have kindly decided that you should be given the opportunity of experiencing love. Does this news make you happy?" John stood up from the chair and raised his hands in the air.

"Am I to be given a second chance at life, oh my God, why me?" he said in a loud excited voice.

"Please sit down again John and let me finish." John sat down feeling the way he used to feel in school when a teacher told him to be quiet.

"You're a bit hard for an angel," said John, feeling annoyed.

"Somebody needs to be firm with you and that job has fallen to me," said Rainbow. This was followed by silence for a few seconds.

"John Hughes's body is dead," continued the angel, "but his soul isn't, though not glowing at present. It was a long meeting that took place, and much thought was given to whether you should or shouldn't be given a second chance. In life, you did not show much feeling towards people. They avoided you. We want you to learn from this. It's a chance to find love, but it's also a chance to see how you wronged others and yourself. It will also be good to watch and see what you make of this opportunity. You are to be given a new identity. From now on, you will be Mark Foynes. You will find yourself calling to this address asking for work." The angel handed him a piece of paper. "There will be a job available for some months, and you will be given that job."

"How can you be sure?" asked John.

"We can make anything happen. We will provide you with an address to say where you have come from and a passport. The foreman won't ask too many questions. That bag behind you contains clothes that will fit you and other essentials. All things are possible here. Nobody will be wronged or hurt by this ruse, and if you do things right this time, you may yet get to taste love in its true form." John felt excited, but he had a lot of questions as to how it would all work out. Before he could ask, Rainbow raised his hand.

"Never mind that," he said, reading John's mind again. "There is however a condition."

"What is it?" The angel stroked his long white beard and leaned forward in the antique armchair. "When, and if you find love and experience that first truly magical feeling, you will have a short time more before we call you back. You will not have to die again but you will find yourself here, and you will have no connection to earth or what happens there from then on." John stood up again and walked around the room. His mind was in a muddle. He didn't like the condition imposed on him, yet he thought it was a chance that probably no one had ever got before.

"You don't have to accept," said Rainbow, looking at the expression on John's face. "If you wish to turn it down, you can proceed on through that green door over there and dwell here forever. Of course, that is after your life review. Everybody has to do that."

"I don't want to think about it anymore, I want to do it, my minds made up." The angel took a light blue envelope from his pocket and handed it to John who suddenly started to shake uncontrollably from head to foot. Rainbow smiled at him.

"As I've already said, you will find everything you want in the bag, passport, essentials etc. You'll find money in the envelope. We also hope you will find love but remember although it will be for a short while only, it will be worth it and if you succeed, you will achieve what you were meant to the first time around on earth. You will not look as you do now, and you will be younger. So, are we agreed about you taking this bold step or do you want to go for your review?" John pressed the envelope against his chest and then shook Rainbow's hand, it was freezing cold.

"Yes," answered John, trying to keep control of himself. "I'm going back to earth."

"Good. Now we have talked enough and I'm terribly busy with other souls today," said the angel. "Close your eyes." John did as he was told, and he felt the cold hand of Rainbow on the top of his head. In an instant, it turned to heat and on opening his eyes he found himself standing in his native Dublin on a nice warm day.

Chapter 2

The Dublin city centre street was busy with traffic and people going in every direction. John was holding a travelling bag with leather handles, the same bag that the angel had pointed to. He remembered the envelope that Rainbow had given him and took it from his pocket. Inside was money and the piece of paper with the address of where he would get work and accommodation. He looked up and saw the name of a small seaside town in North County Dublin on the bus stop. It was the same town to where he was to go to get work. The name was unusual it was called Risk. He'd heard of it before but had never been there. He wondered what his new life would be like and would the name of the town be relatable to his situation. He was standing with his back to a large shop window, and he turned around to look at his reflection. It felt very peculiar seeing a stranger aged about twenty-five looking back at him.

The screeching brakes of a bus pulling in brought his attention back to what he was to do next, and he boarded and paid his fare. He went upstairs and sat in the front seat looking out at everything around him. He had a strong urge to tell everybody on the bus about what had happened to him. It moved off slowly, and John watched from the window at the buildings he was now passing by. Everything fascinated him, even the cars bumper to bumper on the busy city street. The bus stopped several times to take on passengers and was soon full. It took an hour to reach the town of Risk. John got off at a stop in the centre of the town close to a large entrance of an old estate. He looked at the high pillars with large granite balls on top. It had wide Iron gates, behind which was a small gate lodge. A long tree lined avenue seemed to be leading somewhere. He wondered who lived there and what they were like. John looked at the note again and continued up the main street, following Rainbow's directions. He took a turn off to the right on to a narrow road that led towards the sea. It looked majestic in the distance with the sun beating down on it. He soon came upon his destination. It was a large yard with the name Phil Clarke & Sons over the entrance. He looked in through the open gates and saw some vans and a lorry loaded with vegetables. Further on down at the rear of the yard, he could see glasshouses with an abundance of tomatoes growing inside them. Under the owner's name, there was a sign saying, Help Wanted, in large white letters. A man, whistling a tune, was sweeping the yard and John called out to him. "Where can I see about getting a job here?" The man stopped sweeping and pointed with his thumb in the direction behind him.

"Try the office. Joe Hammond is the foreman, and he does all the hiring and firing for Phil Clarke, the owner." John thanked him and walked towards the office. He knocked on the shabby door and a gruff voice from within told him to come in. It was a small room with a lot of dockets and bills strewn across a dark wooden desk that was badly scratched. There was a strong smell of soup and banana sandwiches. Sitting at the desk and almost totally obscured by a pile of paper and small tomato baskets, sat a man who looked like he was in his sixties. His face was red, and he was drinking tea from a chipped cup with red rings around it. He looked over the heap of paper as the door closed behind John.

"Who are you?" he said in an unfriendly tone. John took an immediate dislike to him. He knew he was being far too sensitive as usual. It was one of the things that he'd hated about himself in life.

"My name is Mark Foynes and I saw your notice outside saying help wanted. I'd be interested in a job and would be prepared to give it my best shot." The tea drinker stood up and looked John up and down. He moved aside some of the paperwork on his desk and told John to come forward and sit down. John sat down, and he thought he saw a faint smile on the other man's lip, but in an instant, it was gone.

"I'm Joe Hammond the foreman here and the manager and everything else except the owner. Maybe someday who knows?" John gave a little smile, but Joe Hammond didn't attempt to smile anymore. He explained to John that the work was hard, and that it was a live-in job so that he could be available if any emergencies arose. John said he had no problem with that. Joe asked to see John's passport and he handed it to the foreman. John thought about how Mark Foynes didn't really exist. It was a very strange feeling.

They spent another twenty minutes talking about the nature of the work. The sour foreman explained that he was just taking him on for a few months and it was cash in hand. John said it suited him at this time to do things that way. Joe Hammond suddenly banged his fist on the desk causing his cup to rattle and topple on the saucer. Luckily, it was now empty.

"I'm happy enough with you, so you're hired. It's hard work and you'll earn your money. Make no mistake about that. Do you have other belongings with you, more clothes etc? That bag doesn't look too big."

"I can send for them, don't worry about that." The words just seemed to burst forth from John, but he felt it was somebody speaking through him. The foreman shouted for someone named Dan, and the man whom John had seen sweeping the yard earlier, came in.

"Yes, Mr Hammond," he said in a timid kind of way. He was told to show John to his new abode over the big stores.

Dan told John to follow him and as he did Joe said, loudly, "I'm taking a gamble on you, Foynes. I'm trusting I'm doing the right thing." John looked back but didn't say anything and then followed the cowering sweeper.

Chapter 3

John was told to go up small narrow stone steps on the side of a whitewashed building and that he would find his room there. He climbed the steps and arrived at a well-worn red door. There was a horseshoe covered in rust hanging over the door and some ivy had grown around it. He turned the dull brass doorknob and went in. The room was dark, and he opened the shabby blue curtains that hung miserably on a dirty window. Immediately, the room was brighter, and having a quick look around, he thought it looked okay. He sat down on the bed, and it felt comfortable. It was a good-sized room with a bed, television, wardrobe, sofa, two armchairs and a small fireplace. There was another door, and on opening it, John discovered a small kitchen with a table and two wooden chairs. Another door off the kitchen led to an even smaller bathroom. He thought about the strangeness of his situation and how, by now he would have been long gone if he'd not been given the opportunity to live again and find love.

After sitting for a few minutes in silence on one of the armchairs, John opened his bag and put the contents into the tall brown dusty wardrobe. It smelt of mothballs. He took the passport out and glanced at the unknown face, name and address on it. He looked in a grubby mirror that hung on the wall and saw the same face as the one on the passport. It made him feel odd and false. A knock came to the door, and he opened it. Outside, Dan was standing with the yard brush in his hand.

"Joe said to let you know that he'll be needing you to load a van which will be here soon. Caroline Finnegan will call to pick up supplies. She lives in the town with her parents, and they have a good-sized shop. They buy from us. I won't be able to help her today and the others that work here aren't around, so it's up to you to help her load up." Between coming up the steps, and saying all this, Dan was breathless.

"Yeah, that's fine, I'll watch out for her." Dan shut the door and John heard him going slowly back down the steps. A minute later, John heard movement in the yard and looking out the window, he saw Joe, Dan and two other men getting into a van and driving off. He went into the kitchen and put the kettle on to make himself cup of tea. It didn't take long to boil and just as he was about to make the tea, he heard an engine in the yard. He opened the door and stood at the top of the steps. A young woman about the same age as he was now, was getting out of a red van with white stripes on the side of it.

"Hello, are you here for the vegetables?" he asked. She turned and looked up at him. She was dressed in a green jumper that was far too big for her and was wearing grey jeans and wellingtons. Her hair was dark brown, and she wore it in a ponytail fashion.

"Who are you?" she asked.

"My name is Mark Foynes," said John as he came down the steps. "I started here today, and I've been told to help you load up, that is if you're Caroline Finnegan." She smiled and told him she was. He shook her hand and noticed she had a firm grip. He thought of Rainbow's hand and how it felt freezing and wrinkled. She pointed out to John where the vegetables were usually stored and backed the van up to a big stone building with two red doors. John opened the bolt to the doors which were not locked. It was stacked high with all sorts of vegetables. They both started to load up the van.

She was quiet at first and John thought she just didn't want to talk. After a few minutes of silence, she suddenly threw a question at him.

"How did you get the job or come to know there was one?" He put down the box he was holding and told her a friend of his had told him there was a job there, and he came in search of it.

"I wanted a change from the city and this nice little town will suit me fine."

"Are you going to live up there?" she asked, pointing towards the red door.

"Yeah, that's my new abode now, do you like it?"

"It's quaint, from here anyway. We better get on with this, I have to hurry back to the shop." They started to speed up the loading and he suddenly started to feel happy. He took note of the feeling, as he hadn't felt that way for a long time.

They finished loading the van and Caroline signed a docket for the goods received. He noticed she was left-handed.

"What's the room like?" she asked, pointing with the pen at the window of his room.

"Come up and I'll show you." She closed the back door of the van and followed John up the steps to the red door.

"After you," he said, pushing the door open and letting Caroline walk in ahead of him. She went in and looked around. She walked slowly to the far side of the room.

"You know," she said, looking up at the ceiling and then at the floor, "I've been driving in and out of this yard for quite a while now and I often wondered what it was like in here. The last person to live here was Luke Flynn. He wasn't friendly and then one day, he just suddenly decided to leave. That's how come you're here. Where did you say you found out about this job?"

"A friend told me."

"You must have given a good interview to be taken straight in off the street or else there's somebody praying for you in heaven." John smiled and thought of Rainbow.

"I bet there is," he said with a distant expression on his face.

"I have to leave now," said Caroline. "I need to get back to the shop. I hope you enjoy working here and that you'll stick around for a while." They were now walking down the steps and she thanked him for his help with the loading of the van.

"Thank you," he said, "I enjoyed the chat." Just as she was about to get into the van, she offered her hand again to shake. He took notice this time of the soft feeling, and also noticed the coolness of it. "Cold hands, warm heart," said John. She didn't say anything and got into the van, smiling. She shut the door.

"Well, I'm sure I'll be seeing you around," he said.

"I'll be here from time to time delivering and collecting. My parent's shop is in the middle of the main street, we live overhead, a bit like you." And she pointed to the steps that led to his room.

"Yeah," he said, feeling amused by her comparison. The engine started, and Caroline drove off, waving to John. He stood there in the yard for a few minutes after she'd gone. It was quiet, and the only sounds were the birds tweeting. He thought of how alone he was, in his job and in his new life. He didn't even have siblings or parents anymore. He thought there was something nice about Caroline and looked forward to meeting her again.

Chapter 4

Saturday morning saw John working in a large glasshouse. He had to work a half-day and then he intended to walk on the beech nearby after his lunch. He wasn't expected to work every Saturday, but there would be times when he'd have to. There was a lot of work to be done with the care of tomatoes in the glasshouses. It was hot work under the glass with the sun beating down. Four hours later, he was back in his new home after having a bath and preparing something to eat. As he sat eating, he got the idea to look up his death notice on the mobile phone that he'd found in the bag that Rainbow had given him. He entered his details and the notice popped up on the screen. It was eerie, he thought, to be reading about his own passing, perhaps even macabre. To him, it read lonely and felt unbearably sad. He couldn't finish reading it, and he quickly came out of the website. It left him feeling depressed and sorry that he'd looked it up. He finished his food and dressed quickly for his walk to the beach. He came out through the small gate as the big ones were now shut for the weekend. He walked on taking note of everything around him. The weather had changed slightly since he was in the glasshouse, and it now felt cold.

The beech was only about ten minutes' walk from where he was staying. He walked down the narrow lane with small trees on either side and found himself on a beautiful long strand facing the wide blue ocean. He walked towards it and watched the waves crashing in, one after another. They were loud in his ears like the booming of cannons. He looked out at an island in the middle of the sea and wondered what it would be like to live there. Looking behind him to his right, he saw sand dunes which went on for a considerable distance. John loved the dunes and he walked quickly towards them like an excited child. There was a small track that twisted between the little sandy hills, and as he walked along, he saw Caroline coming towards him. He waved to her, and she waved back, giving him a big smile. She was wearing a long black coat.

"Fancy meeting you here," he said, as he got nearer to her.

"I often walk here on Saturdays and other days when I get a chance. There's nothing unusual in that. I'm on my way back to the shop. Are you not working today?" she asked.

"I was this morning for a few hours, in one of the glasshouses. They're hot places to work in." She laughed and told him he just wasn't used to it yet.

"I suppose you're right. Well, I'll let you finish your walk and get back to the shop."

"What are you doing later?" she asked.

"Nothing, I don't know, I'm new here and I don't know the best places to go. Mind you, this beach is hard to beat."

"There's a band playing tonight in Fairley's, that's a big pub in the town with a dance floor. Anything goes really. People put up requests and they dance, sing and I suppose fall in love, sometimes. Anyway, I'm going there later with two friends. If you want to meet up with us, you're more than welcome. We'll be there about nine."

"I might just do that. I think I saw that place on the way into town. It looks okay. Will I have trouble getting in or do I need a ticket or something?"

"No, but they still ask for a small cover charge sometimes. If you've any problems getting in, just mention my name and they'll come to me. Look at the time it is," she said, suddenly checking her gold wristwatch. "See you later, that is if you come of course. Anyway, enjoy the rest of your walk, sorry I have to rush."

He watched her hurrying away through the dunes in the direction of the lane. He turned and walked on further, thinking about what Caroline had said about people falling in love. He couldn't get it out of his head. He hadn't ever experienced falling in love except maybe very early on in life, but then that was short lived all those years ago. He sat down on one of the dunes and looked out at the island and at the clouds moving above it. He thought about his life before this one. He pictured his family around his hospital bed as he lay dying. It caused him to shudder.

"This is the strangest thing that's ever happened to me," he said out loud, as there was nobody around. He wanted to tell somebody what had happened to him. It was lonely, and he didn't feel like he was anybody.

"Who is Mark Foynes?" he asked himself. "As this man, I have no history, no family, nothing. I am a creation, just like in one of those Frankenstein films. I have actually passed through death and come back again. Who would believe it?" He thought about Rainbow and what he'd said about how it was a chance for John to find what had eluded him the first time around. It all sounded crazy, but this was how it was, and John reminded himself again of why he was there.

Chapter 5

Later that evening, John stood in front of the mirror shaving himself. The razor made a low rasping sound as he dragged it through the shaving foam. He washed his face, changed his clothes, and sat down to have something to eat. He glanced at the clock and saw the time was moving on, so having rushed his tea, he put on his jacket and went outside. It was a nice mild night, and not a leave stirred on the tall trees outside the gate. He locked the door behind him. Just before he took the key from the lock, he got a feeling that he should touch the horseshoe that hung overhead. This he did and then hurried down the steps. He looked around the yard, checking to see if everything was secure. As he lived in the yard, he was responsible for making sure it was secure at night.

Six minutes later he was walking through the door of Fairley's. It was a big place with tables and seats surrounding a wooden dance floor. Around the walls hung old lanterns, swords and antique pictures. Close to the bar counter was an old mill wheel. It was turning in the floor. Water poured down from the ceiling and the revolving wheel caused the floor to vibrate. John thought it a very different kind of pub, and he liked it.

"Mark, Mark, over here." Looking around, he saw Caroline waving to him from a corner where she was sitting. He crossed the floor and came up to her table. She was with two friends.

"This is Fionula and Sheila, this is Mark," she said introducing them to each other. He shook their hands and Caroline moved in further on the leather seat so that he could sit down. She was wearing a plaid shirt and jeans.

"Mark here is the new man in Phil Clarke's yard," said Caroline to explain who exactly this stranger was that was joining them. Fionula giggled.

"I don't envy you working with Joe Hammond, he can be a bit cross, isn't that right, Sheila?"

"Yeah," replied Sheila, "but I think his bark is worse than his bite."

"I'm glad to hear it," said John, "I haven't had many dealings with him yet, but he's keeping me busy. He's got a driving job for me on Monday. I've got to pick up something in Dublin, so we'll see how that goes." It went quiet for a few seconds and John was wracking his brain in search of what to say next. Sheila asked him where he'd worked before coming to Risk.

"I was working in a small food warehouse in the city centre, Whelehan's," he replied. "It was a good place to work, but I needed a change. So, I'm still in the same line really." They all agreed, and John ordered a drink from the barmaid who now stood at their table with a tray in her hand.

The evening went on and they all enjoyed themselves. Fionula was very witty, and she made John laugh several times over the course of the night. Caroline seemed to him to be the independent type, but good fun to be with. Sheila was a little bit deep and seemed to look through him. He felt she gave him an occasional searching glance over the evening. He could see in her eyes that she wanted to know more about him. In short, he decided that she was suffering a bit with curiosity, but nice really. Then he began to wonder if she was interested in him in another way. They all danced together over the course of the evening, and no more questions were asked.

Later, Fionula and Sheila went to the toilets and John was sitting alone with Caroline. He decided to ask her straight out if she'd like to come out again some evening.

"Yes, that would be nice, I'd like that," was her quick reply. "Give me a call." She scribbled down her mobile number and handed it to him. He looked at it and then put it into his shirt pocket.

"Okay," he said, "I'll call you on Tuesday evening."

Shortly afterwards they all decided to leave. He walked them home, as they lived nearby. They didn't delay and were gone quickly as he left each one at their home. Caroline was the last to leave and touched John on the arm saying that she would listen out for his call. He said goodnight and left her at her parent's shop.

The night had now turned chilly, and he hurried towards the yard. He went in through the small gate and turned on the yard light. All was silent, and he turned it off again. He had left the small light on over his door so that he could see the steps as he ascended. He turned the key and went in. He compared the quietness and lonely feeling with the crowded Fairley's. He put the kettle on and sat down. John wondered what future there was in any of it and where he was going. A few minutes later, the kettle clicked off and he made himself tea and a cheese sandwich. It was a solitary supper, but he enjoyed it and thought about how the evening had gone. Not too long afterwards, John went to bed. As he lay under the blankets instead of a mound of clay, he wondered was he really fortunate and where his new life would take him. "So many thoughts," he said out loud and minutes later, he was soundly asleep.

Chapter 6

Monday morning came, and John was up early ready to meet the new week. He had a quick breakfast and hurried down to Joe Hammond's office. Just as he was about to knock, the door opened, and Joe appeared looking sour as usual.

"You want me to go to Dublin today," said John. The foreman looked at him.

"Yeah, that's right, I want you call to that address" – he handed John a dirty scrap of paper – "and pick up a machine part. Ask for Des and tell him I sent you. He's expecting you, oh and by the way did you finish that job in the glasshouse last Saturday?"

"I got it all done."

"Good," said Joe. "You might have noticed I didn't ask you for a reference for this job. I don't bother too much with that sort of thing, and I like to make up my own mind about someone. Don't let me down and we should have no problems." John said he wouldn't.

"So why are you still standing here then?" said Joe. "Go to Dublin and get that part and don't take all day about it."

A few minutes later, John was on his way into the city. It was a nice bright day, and there were small fluffy clouds in the blue sky. They reminded him of angels, and he thought of Rainbow. He pulled into a filling station just outside Risk and treated himself to a coffee and chocolate bar. He felt good to be alive again and on the road. There was a magical if lonely feeling to it all. He started the van again and drank the coffee as he drove along.

An hour later, he arrived in Dublin and went in the direction of Capel Street, as that was where he was to pick up the part. He soon found the address and was lucky to get a parking space right outside the entrance. He went inside and asked at the reception for Des. It was an old building and smelt musty. Des, a stocky built man came out from an office, and John told him that Joe Hammond had sent him for the part.

"Come with me," said Des, and John followed him out of the building and up a cobbled lane to the left of the entrance.

"That's it," said Des, pointing to a piece of machinery. Between them, they placed the heavy part in a wheelbarrow and brought it to the van. They struggled to get it out again and in doing so, John cut his hand. He noticed there was no blood. "I suppose I don't have blood in me because I'm not alive anymore, I'm not real," he said to himself. Des hadn't noticed John cutting himself and was breathless trying to lift the part out of the wheelbarrow. They eventually managed to get it into the van but with great difficulty, and it was safely stored. John got back into the van and Des waved him off. John drove down a side street to take a short cut, when suddenly he saw his brother, Michael coming from the opposite direction. He wanted to jump out of the van and hug him, but he knew his brother wouldn't recognise him now. As Michael drew nearer, John felt himself shaking with a heaving emotion within him. He wanted to know how his family were doing. He wondered if they were coming to terms with his death or if they'd forgotten him already.

Michael passed the van and was walking briskly along the street. John got out of the van and followed him. He didn't know why or what he intended to do. Michael turned a corner and John stopped. He knew it would do no good. To Michael he was dead and gone forever. John felt like a cheat. He was overpowered with feelings of sadness, loss and guilt. His eyes started to sting him, and he walked slowly back to the van feeling rage growing inside him. He sat in the driving seat banging the steering wheel in anger and staring blankly at the car parked in front of him. Eventually, he turned the key in the engine and said out loud, "What's the point." He drove back to his fake life in Risk. As he drove, he noticed the cut on his hand had disappeared.

Chapter 7

Tuesday evening, John called Caroline. The phone was answered with a friendly hello. "Do you have any plans this Saturday afternoon? I'm off for the whole day?" said John.

"The weather is supposed to be good, maybe we could walk out to the old Martello tower on the coast. It's a lovely spot for picnics. I've been there lots of times, it's a favourite place of mine."

"I'd like that," said John, "I think I can just about see the tower from my window. It's in Loughsane, isn't it?"

"Yeah, it's a really lovely place. Okay so. I'll meet you outside Clarke's gate on Saturday about two o' clock. If there's any change, give me a call."

"Okay," said John, "I'm looking forward to it. I'll bring some cake and something to drink."

"That would be nice, see you then." And Caroline hung up. There was a knock at the door. John answered it and found Dan outside.

"You still here?" said John. Dan said yeah but that he had something to finish, and that Joe had asked him to tell Mark something when he got back.

"Oh," said John, "what could that be?"

"There's a girl starting in the office next Monday. She'll be tidying up all that mess in there and all I can say is, God help her. I hope she's patient."

"Why is Joe bothering to tell me, what's it to me who he takes on?" asked John, curiously.

"Because," said Dan with a grin on his narrow-pinched face, "he wants you to help her out, along with your own work. I wish you well." And he walked away, laughing. John closed the door and sat down in an armchair. He told himself he didn't care and so what, he'd done work like that before. To him it was nothing compared to being dead. He quickly put it out of his head and his thoughts switched to the coming Saturday.

Chapter 8

For the rest of the week, John worked hard on a range of jobs. He liked to keep busy as it took his mind off his strange situation. When Friday afternoon came, he was called to the office to talk to Joe Hammond about some unpaid bills. He sat opposite Joe, and they went through bundles of dog-eared invoices and dockets that lay on the desk.

"I hear there's a new girl starting in the office," said John, trying to make out the faded writing on one of the bills.

"Yeah, I have her name here somewhere, let me see." Joe rummaged through some envelopes on a tray. "Here it is. She's called Ronna Smyth, and she's got a lot of experience. Phil Clarke and I interviewed her last week in Phil's other place. She comes well recommended. As I told you before, I like to make up my own mind about people. Clarke was impressed by her and her experience, so we're taking her on." John asked if it was true that he was expected to work with Ronna Smyth.

"Yes, from time to time. There's a huge filing job coming up and I want you both to work together on it. I know you're busy, but I also know you're a good worker and that you can do this. We can't ask Dan; he'd be lost at something like that and probably make a mess of it into the bargain."

Shortly after, John left the office and looked at his watch, it was nearly finishing time. He was about to mount the stairs to his room when he heard beeping. He looked towards the gate and saw Caroline waving to him from the van. He walked across the yard, and she rolled down the window.

"How would this evening suit you instead of tomorrow? It's going to be a bit awkward for me then, I'm afraid."

"Great, that's okay with me. I'd still like to go to Loughsane though. We could have our picnic in the van and then go for that walk up to the Martello tower," Caroline said she'd like that and as it would be too cold to sit out on the grass in the evening, she would be happy to picnic in the van.

"Can you come back in an hour, if that's okay with you?" he asked.

"Okay, I'll see you here in an hour. Don't be late." She drove off and John climbed the steps to his lodgings. He put the kettle on to make himself a quick cup of tea. While it was boiling, he shaved and found himself lost in thought as he brought the razor gently down his foamed cheeks. Shaving always had this effect on him, but now it wasn't simply daydreaming. The face being shaved and looking back at him was not his face. When his eyes met the eyes in the mirror, John felt he was looking at a shell. There was no light in them. They were empty. He had no background now, no history, no parents, no experiences, and a hollow feeling inside him. Mark Foynes simply did not exist and never had.

"Stop, stop," he said to himself, and he rinsed the remaining lather from his face. He took a cake, bottle of wine and two glasses out of the fridge and put them into a bag. He made himself a quick cup of tea and sat down waiting anxiously for Caroline.

Not long afterwards, he heard the familiar beep of the van, and he hurried out to meet her. He got into the van, and they were soon on the road to Loughsane.

"It's not far, we should be there in about fifteen minutes," said Caroline, cheerfully. She noticed John's bag. "What's in there?"

"Cake, wine and two glasses."

"Yum yum," she said, "I better watch what I drink, having to drive and all that." They both laughed, and John started to feel his spirts lifting again. He was sitting in a van with a girl whom he liked, and they were heading off to a romantic spot.

"Is this what love feels like?" he asked himself. Before he had time to think anymore, they arrived at the little carpark at Loughsane harbour. Caroline produced a small picnic basket from the back seat that contained some nice surprises, and together they tucked in. John opened the wine and filled the two glasses.

"Not too much for me," said Caroline, "remember, I'm driving. I'll have to sip it slowly."

When they'd finished, they decided to walk to the Martello tower. On the way, John spotted a tall white lighthouse with black rings painted around it. He loved lighthouses and had always been fascinated by them. "I'd love to see inside that lighthouse," he said, pointing towards it. Caroline smiled at him.

"It just so happens a friend of mine, Clair Frawley lives there. She's an actress and reads palms in her spare time. It's not a functioning lighthouse anymore and hasn't been for about thirty years. Clair moved in about five years ago and loves living there. Come on, she'll let you see inside." John followed her up the hill to the lighthouse and the door opened. A woman aged about thirty stood in front of them. John thought there was something bohemian about her. She wore a long black dress and had a purple scarf around her neck. Her face was very pale, and it stood out in contrast with the clothes she wore.

"Hi, Clair," said Caroline and they hugged each other. "This is Mark, a friend of mine, he's working in Clarkes. He loves lighthouses."

"Hello, Mark," said Clair in a slow voice, "I saw you both from the top window as you were approaching, come in." They followed her in and up winding steps that led to a round room. Pictures of theatres and lighthouses adorned the thick walls. John and Caroline sat down on a large pink sofa and Clair sat opposite them on an armchair. Caroline asked Clair if she was acting in anything at the moment.

"I'm supposed to be starting in a play next month, so I'm looking over my script and of course reading the odd palm when people call to me."

"How exciting," said Caroline, "would you like to read Mark's palm?"

"Oh, I'm sure Clair is busy learning her lines," said John, "maybe another time."

"Nonsense," said Caroline, "go on be a devil, you mightn't be up this way again for a long time. Go on, I'd love to see what your palm says." John felt himself growing nervous.

"You don't have to if you don't want to, Mark," said Clair noticing his unease.

"Don't worry," said Caroline, "you should see your face. What harm can it do?" John agreed reluctantly and held out his hand. Clair took it in hers and looked at the lines on his palm. She didn't say anything for a few minutes and moved his hand in different directions.

"This is very strange," she said, "there's nothing in the lines on your palm. It's as though you've never lived. It's not possible. I'll try concentrating on your name, what is it?"

"Mark Foynes." Clair put her hand on his forehead and closed her eyes for a few moments. She opened them again and took her hand away. "I don't understand what's happening, I'm getting a psychic impression saying there is no Mark Foynes. I'm sorry I can't tell you anymore. This has never happened before. I'm sure there must be some explanation, never mind, would you like some tea?"

"No, thank you," John answered quickly. He was anxious to leave and stood up to go. Caroline stood up and said they'd have tea the next time they called.

"Oh well," said Clair, "until the next time then. I promise I won't try to read your palm again, Mark." He smiled at her and left with Caroline who was looking very perplexed.

They walked back to the car and got in. Caroline put the key in the ignition but didn't turn it. She looked hard at John.

"What, why are you looking at me like that?" he asked. "Surely, you don't believe all that mumbo jumbo."

"It just so happens I do," said Caroline in an angry voice. "I have the greatest respect for Clair and her gift. I've had my palm read by her several times, and she's always been very accurate. There's something you're not telling me. If you're not Mark Foynes, who are you?" John didn't answer her and looked out the window.

"Please look at me and tell me if you are really Mark Foynes." John turned towards Caroline and looked her straight in the eye. He couldn't answer her.

"So, it's true then. Am I safe with you?" she asked. "Are you on the run or something? Please tell me what's going on."

"If I told you, you wouldn't believe me. I can't say anything more just for now, maybe sometime in the future." Caroline grew impatient and started the engine. They sat for a few minutes and didn't say anything. She was the one to break the silence.

"I can't help feeling something illegal is going on with you. I'm not going to be involved in whatever it is, so for that reason we won't be meeting each other outside of work in the future." She drove the car back towards Risk and John didn't speak on the journey.

They arrived at Clarke's gate and John got out. He hesitated and said before shutting the door of the car, "I have done nothing illegal, believe me."

"That may or may not be true, but you can't tell me who you really are. How can I be with someone like that?"

"Someday, maybe I will be able to, I'm sorry." He shut the door and turned towards the gate. He looked back and saw her looking in the mirror at him before driving away. He opened the small gate in the large one and went in. All was quiet, and he stood looking at the place where he had helped Caroline to load the van not so long ago. He remembered how he'd enjoyed her company that day. He went up to his lonely room and sat down on the sofa. All sorts of thoughts passed through his mind as he sat there in silence. Rainbow's face came into his mind, and he wondered was there a way of asking him for assistance.

After sitting for twenty minutes wondering what to do, he decided he would ask for help. He turned out the light, lit a candle and sat opposite it. John closed his eyes and tried to picture Rainbow talking to him. He formed the angel's face in his mind's eye and tried hard to hold the focus. It was difficult, but he managed to keep the image in his mind.

"Hello again," said a familiar voice. John opened his eyes and Rainbow was sitting opposite him in his long brown linen coat with silver buttons. "Don't look so surprised, you called me, didn't you, and I'm here. I know what has happened." John looked at the angel who was now smiling in a kind way.

"What do I do?" asked John. "I like Caroline, but now she's on to me, knows I'm not completely straight with her. I'm afraid she'll say something, and I'll lose my job. Maybe it's time for me to give up on this and go back with you. I feel I'm living a lie." Rainbow was running his fingers through his long beard while John spoke but stopped and gave John a serious look. "The lie was the life you led in your other life. It was a lie to yourself and cost you your happiness. Have you ever heard of spirit guides?" he asked. John said he had but wasn't sure if he believed such beings existed.

"Well, I must say that's a laugh," said Rainbow. "You believe in me don't you and how do you think you got back here? You have a spirit guide called Emma," continued the ancient angel. "She has lived a human life before. That's the difference between guides and angels. We have never had an earthly existence. For that reason, it would be good for you to meet Emma and you would feel you have something in common. She will know about the trials and tribulations of life. You can call on her whenever you want. It's easy for you to make contact because, if you remember, you are dead already or did you forget?"

"Sometimes I do, I suppose I don't like to think of myself as being dead. I try to block the thought of it every time I look in the mirror."

"You've been given a rare second chance," said Rainbow, "putting it that way doesn't sound too bad, does it? Spend the next few hours thinking it over. Go for a walk on the beach, stay here in the quiet of your room, or go for a cup of coffee somewhere. Think hard about your situation and if you want, you can call Emma. That is my advice to you now." Suddenly, Rainbow was gone, and John sat looking at an empty space. He went out to the front door and looked up at the vastness of the sky. He touched the horseshoe over the door. The cold feeling from it reminded him of his first meeting with

Rainbow. He went back into his small home and grabbed his coat. He decided he would go for a walk on the beach. A few minutes later as he walked down the narrow lane, he made up his mind that he would try to contact his spirit guide, Emma. He wondered what she looked like and what she would say to him.

Chapter 9

Monday morning came and John was driving a tractor in the fields. He found working on the land made him happy, and he felt at one with nature. Birds followed the tractor as he turned the rich earth. They swooped down in search of worms now exposed by the turned soil. It was a bright sunny day, and he tried not to think of anything except the work he was engaged in.

At one o' clock, he was back in the yard and ready to have lunch in his little abode. As he ascended the steps, he heard Joe Hammond calling him.

"Yeah," answered John, "I'm just going to have my lunch break, is everything all right?"

"Come in here for a minute, I want you to meet our new member of staff," replied the usually grumpy foreman. John noticed how Joe wasn't as sour today and thought to himself, "that's because he's trying to impress the new girl."

John came back down the steps and crossed the yard to the office. The door was open, and he walked in. Joe was sitting forward in the chair with his fingers tapping impatiently on the desk.

"This is Ronna Smyth, she's starting right away," said Joe, waving his hand in the direction of the new recruit. John walked towards her, and she stood up and shook hands. She was aged about twenty-five and was dressed in a light blue jacket with a matching skirt. She was pretty with fair hair and a broad smile. She seemed friendly and had a capable confident air about her.

"Pleased to meet you," said Ronna, "I'm told that we'll be working together from time to time. I look forward to that." And she nodded her head, slightly.

"I'm Mark, and yes I look forward to working with you too. I'm around here a lot if you need help with finding anything."

"Okay that's all," said Joe, "go and have your lunch now." Ronna thanked John, and he left the office. He went to his room and had a sandwich and tea while reading a small novel he'd found at the back of the wardrobe. He heard somebody driving into the yard and wondered who it was. He looked out the window and saw Caroline's van, but she wasn't driving it. A man, who John guessed must be her father, got out. He was tall and broad with a blue peaked cap on his head. He started to load up some boxes with Dan and Sean, another worker there. They didn't take long, and the two helpers went off to do another job. Joe Hammond came out of the office and started talking to Caroline's father.

"Well, Jack, it's all there, just sign that for me," said Joe, handing him a docket and pen. Jack took the pen and scribbled his name.

"How is that daughter of yours, Caroline, I thought she'd be coming to collect this lot? I haven't seen you in the yard for a long time now."

"Ah, she's okay," replied Jack. "I think she was a bit sweet on that new worker you have here."

"Oh, you mean Mark," said Joe. "He's okay, keeps to himself. When he's not working, he's either in his room or walking on the beach. I didn't know there was something going on between him and Caroline."

"Well," said Jack, "I don't think there is now. She was to go on some sort of a picnic and then for some reason, she came home early and not looking very happy either. I didn't find out anything and neither has Grace. We're just wondering what happened. What do you know about him? I don't want him upsetting Caroline." Joe scratched his head and looked up towards John's door as if checking not to be overheard. John was hiding behind the lace curtain and had the window slightly ajar. He could make out every word they were saying.

"Mark's a good worker," said Joe. "I'm happy enough with him. It's not a job that's going to last long. Look, between ourselves, he appeared at the gate one day and I took him on. He had a previous address and a passport and that was good enough for me. As I said, the job is of short duration, and he'll be gone soon. I didn't take him on through the proper channels, but he was happy with the arrangement. I got a good feeling about him and that's good enough for me. I've no interest in what he does in his spare time. As long as he gets the job done, I'm happy."

"I better go, Joe, I'm running late. Maybe it was a lover's tiff or something, but I think it'll probably mean that I'll be coming into the yard for a while instead of Caroline." They both laughed and Jack got into the van and drove off. John came down the steps and Joe asked him had he cleared the bags of weeds from the far field.

"I'm just going to finish it off now."

"Leave that until tomorrow," said Joe. "Ronna needs you to work with her on those invoices and dockets. It's a huge job. I have to go into town. I'll get Dan to clear the bags. She's in the office now, go straight into her, she'll be glad of your help."

John walked towards the office and Joe shouted to him that he'd be back about 5 o' clock.

"Okay," said John, "see you then." He watched Joe driving away and then turned towards the door of the office. Just as he was about to go in, he heard crying coming from inside. He hesitated for a few seconds and then turned the doorknob, slowly.

Chapter 10

On entering, John heard a bustling sound and saw Ronna trying to busy herself as if trying to throw off any suspicions he had. He stood in front of the shabby desk where she sat and looked at her. Her face was red, and she'd obviously been crying.

"What's wrong?" he asked, as he sat down on the chair opposite her. She looked away and said there was nothing wrong.

"Then why are there tears on your cheeks?" She quickly rubbed them off with the back of her hand and looked embarrassed.

"That's better," he said. "Tell me what's wrong, maybe I can help. Is it Joe, or are you feeling maybe that this job is not for you after all?"

"No," replied Ronna, trying hard not to start crying again. "I'm only starting the job as you know, but I'm not worried about it, or Joe either. I've got you to help me sometimes or, so I've been told. I don't live too far away and getting here is not a problem. All is okay on that score."

"On that score maybe, but why were you crying just now?" She pushed the chair back a bit from the desk and took a deep breath. She didn't say anything for a few seconds. John started to wonder if he was annoying her.

"I was crying," she said, "because not too long ago, my brother, Peter, died. He just came to mind as I sat here on my own. That often happens when I'm alone. We were very close, and I was devastated at his passing as were the rest of my family. I had great faith up to then and it's always been a comfort to me. When Peter died, I just had to know he'd gone somewhere, and I asked him to send me a sign. Please don't think I'm being ridiculous." John thought of his own death and his grieving family and wondered if they were upset like Ronna.

"Don't laugh," she continued, "when I tell you this, but when we were children, we were out walking one day, and Peter found a large white feather with a black tip. He used to put it in his hair and played cowboys and Indians when he was with his friends. The feather fascination wore off over the years as these things do when we grow up. He did love it though, and I thought maybe if I asked for a sign that he's somewhere now, I could be happy again. I asked him to send me a feather but there's been nothing. I know it sounds stupid and silly, but I'm now beginning to wonder if there really is anything after we die." Tears started to appear in her eyes again and she sounded heartbroken. John felt he now had some experience in this area and wanted to help her.

"Don't cry, Ronna, maybe Peter just hasn't heard you yet."

She looked up in puzzlement. "What do you mean?" she asked. "I don't understand."

"Okay, look at it this way," said John, "I think these things will happen when the time is right and not before. Who knows where your brother is at this stage, or maybe he's not yet in a position to send you a sign?"

"Are you serious?" she asked, looking astonished and desperately hopeful at the same time.

"Yes, I'm serious. Let's wait and see. In the meantime, try not to dwell on it for the sake of your peace of mind. Now, we have a lot of work ahead of us, so let's get a start on this mountain of paper or we'll both be sacked."

She moved closer to the desk and looked John straight in the eye. "Thank you so much," she said, touching his arm, "I knew the first moment I met you that you were very nice." John smiled, and they began to wade through the bundles of dockets and letters that lay scattered in front of them.

Chapter 11

Later that evening, John was at home having something to eat and watching television. He and Ronna had worked hard for several hours on the huge amount of paperwork and had only scratched the surface. They had made a good start into it, but there was still an awful lot to be done. John had told Ronna that he wouldn't be working with her the next day as he had a lot of work to catch up on in the glasshouses in the north field. She had decided to stay at it for a while longer and he left her in the office.

He now sat drinking tea in his small sitting room and thinking about Ronna and her brother. He wanted to help her and decided to call on Rainbow. He closed his eyes and called the angel with his mind. There was no answer, and Rainbow did not come. John felt let down and couldn't understand why he was being ignored. He started to think about everything. He liked Caroline, but he hadn't heard from her since. He also felt a bond with Ronna. "Is this what love is?" he asked himself. "Is it normal to have conflicting thoughts and feelings, indeed is it right?" He was confused and felt at a loss. It seemed his path to finding love would not be straight. Ronna's face sprang back into his minds-eye again. At the same time, he thought about the difference between himself and Caroline. "What can I tell her?" he asked himself. "She'd never believe me and who would, it sounds so absurd?"

He stood up, feeling despair coming over him and turned off the television. He sat down again and sighed. He began to feel sleepy and started to doze off.

"Hello," came a voice and opening his eyes, John saw a woman sitting in the corner of the room. She wore a long white dress and had dark hair, split down the middle, brought back on either side, and tied at the back. She sat very straight, and her eyes were strangely bright. It was more like a dazzling whiteness.

"You know who I am, don't you?" she said in a gentle musical voice.

"Am I right in thinking that you are Emma, my spirit guide?" he asked.

"Yes," she replied, "you know you are. You've been calling Rainbow but he's busy, and anyway it's time now that we met in person. Being dead you know, allows you to have this contact easily. Isn't it wonderful? Most people would not be able to see their guide unless they were dead or gifted in some way. I know you have questions and I'm happy to answer them." John walked towards her and touched her shoulder.

"Yes, I'm real," she said smiling, "you of all people should know that." He felt embarrassed, as if he'd offended her.

"It's okay, you don't have to feel bad," said Emma. "Don't forget I can read your mind. Do you know," she continued, "I think it might be a good idea if I told you about my own life here on earth. It might help us to understand each other better. What do you say to that?"

"Yes, I'd love to hear about your time on earth, but I'm more concerned about Ronna now and I want to help her."

"There's no need for you to worry," said Emma. "She'll find the feather she wants so badly in the top drawer of the desk where I put it. Her brother will send her another sign sometime later when he can. It's just not possible for him at the moment."

"Oh, thank you, thank you," said John. "That will mean so much to her." Emma smiled at him. She took his hand and led him to the table.

"Sit down here near me," she said. "You're going to get to know me better." He moved his chair and sat beside her. She placed her hands flat on her lap as if to prepare herself. "Life is a fascinating journey as you know," she began. "It takes us in all directions, throws obstacles in our way and at the same time presents opportunities. I worked for a family in a very big house. I looked after the children's education, and, on occasion did other tasks when needed. I enjoyed my work there and it was close to my home. I lived in during the week, but was at home with my parents, brothers and sisters at the weekends. The work was hard sometimes, but I liked it. I was happy." She went silent for a minute and John waited to see what was coming next. She smiled and started again. "A man started working in the stables, his name was Patrick Grimes. We liked each other and soon we were keeping company together. Patrick's father had an inn, and, on his death, he left it to Patrick. Patrick left working in the stables of the big house and shortly afterwards we were married. I went to live over the inn, and I helped him to run it. Our time together was cut short when one day while I was in the stable at the inn doing something. I was bending down behind a horse when suddenly it kicked out and hit me full force in the head. I really don't remember much after that. I was unconscious for a long time, and then I opened my eyes again and saw Patrick at my bedside. It was lovely to see him there even if we were both so sad. You didn't have that did you John? There wasn't that special person there to say goodbye to you."

John wanted to answer her, but he couldn't get the words out.

"Don't say anything just yet," she said reading his mind again. "I died soon after that and went to the great beyond. I had my review and met Patrick when he crossed over many years later. I had all that you hadn't. I know your story well. I chose to become a spirit guide, and I chose you as someone to watch out for. You were eleven years old when I was assigned to you. You were good in your early life, but after you were thirteen you didn't always listen to your heart. Lots of people do that, some early on and some later in life. I tried hard to guide you without interfering with your freewill. You let a hardness and unhappiness take root in your soul and your head. I want you to think about that." She stopped suddenly and then folded her long arms.

"You've met your spirit guide," she said smiling, "not many do. Just know that I will be with you all the time. Very soon, there will be a knock at the door." When she said this, it felt like she was suddenly changing the subject. John heard running up the steps outside. Emma disappeared and at the same time there was loud knocking at the door. He could hear Ronna calling him.

"Are you there, Mark? Open the door. I've got something to tell you, to show you." He opened the door and Ronna was standing outside holding a large white feather with a black tip.

Chapter 12

"Look," said Ronna, in a state of extreme excitement. She hurried in past John, and he shut the door behind her.

"I opened the drawer in the desk and there it was, the sign that I asked for." She held the feather up high between her slender fingers.

"Well, that's great, now you know that your brother is somewhere." He gave her a reassuring tap on the arm but noticed her tensing up.

"What's the matter?" asked John. She looked at the feather and then back at him. "You put it there, didn't you?"

"No," he replied, "I didn't, it wasn't me." Ronna was quiet for a moment.

"Come on, tell the truth, you put it there." John gave her a cross look.

"I did not put the feather in the drawer."

"I believe you," she said, "I know by the look on your face, yet I feel you know something about it. It happened after we spoke and nobody else knew except you." John tried to act casual, "Maybe your brother has heard you at last. Isn't it great, why question it?" Ronna gave him a knowing kind of smile and was about to say something, when suddenly a text came through on John's phone.

"I'll talk to you later," said Ronna and she hurried away. John read the text which had come from Caroline. In it, she said how she missed him, but she couldn't be with somebody who kept secrets from her. She told him that the ball was now in his court, and that he should tell her who he really was. He walked out to the steps that led to his room and stood there looking at the trees outside the gate. After a few minutes, he grew restless, went inside again, and sat down. He remained sitting for an hour just staring at the floor and then reached for his mobile phone. He sent Caroline a text saying, he could meet her on Saturday at 2pm at the sand dunes where he would tell her what she wanted to know. His hand shook as he typed out the message, and he wondered if it was all right with Rainbow to do this. John hesitated and then hit the send button saying out loud, "There, it's gone now for better or worse." He went into the bathroom and soaped his face for a shave. He looked again at the stranger's reflection looking back at him and thought it was a good face, a kind face. He dragged the razor across his stubble and was lost in thought as he shaved. He was thinking about his family, Caroline, Ronna and the whole new life that he was now living. He went over everything in his head, and it all seemed crazy to him. "Back from the dead, a new identity, a chance to find love, who on earth would believe it?" he asked himself. Sometimes it all felt too much for him and his head felt ready to explode. He tried hard to think of something lovely happening and pictured a huge red love heart beating inside him. The image helped him to feel positive and he decided to use it in the future whenever he felt down.

His phone bleeped. He picked it up and read the message. It was from Caroline. She agreed to meet him at the time and place that he had said. He threw the phone on the sofa and decided to try and think no more about it until Saturday.

Chapter 13

Saturday came around quickly, and John was on his way to the sand dunes for his appointment with Caroline. As he walked down the narrow sandy lane, birds tweeted in the bushes on either side. It all seemed lovely and simple and just for that moment, everything seemed beautiful to him.

He reached the end of the lane and saw that the tide was fully in. A family were walking on the beach, and the children skipped along playfully ahead of their parents. John took a deep breath, held it for as long as he could and then exhaled slowly. It had an up-lifting effect on him. He turned to his right and saw Caroline standing on top of the dunes. She stood out against the sky like a beacon, and the clouds moved swiftly overhead. He waved to her, but she didn't wave back. He waved again and this time she waved. John crossed the beach and climbed to the spot where she was standing. She was wearing her long black coat and a red wool hat.

"Are you long here?" he asked, as he reached the top.

"No, I've just arrived. Looks like it's turning into a windy day."

"Do you want to go somewhere else, maybe that small café in the centre of town?" said John.

"No," she answered, sharply, "I'm happy enough here. There's a more sheltered place on further, it's just a little further on, it won't take us long to get there." They walked on and neither of them spoke until they reached the spot. It was secluded and the surrounding dense growth protected them from the wind.

"This is it," said Caroline and she sat down on the sand. John sat beside her and took two chocolate bars from his pocket. He handed one to her.

"Thanks for that, I like chocolate," she said, taking it quickly from him. They ate the bars and engaged in small talk about the weather and work etc. The chocolate was soon gone, and John stood up, took a few steps away from Caroline and looked out at the sea.

"You're anxious about telling me whatever it is that you're hiding, aren't you?" she said. He turned around and walked back over to where she was and sat down again.

"You won't believe what I'm going to tell you, nobody would, but it's true."

"Try me," she said. "Whatever it is, please tell me it's nothing illegal or that you're not in trouble with the law. If it is anything like that, I just want to leave here right now." John smiled at her and told her not to worry, that he hadn't broken the law and wasn't in any trouble of that kind.

"Well then," said Caroline with a sound of impatience in her voice, "what is it that you're struggling to tell me?" John told her everything from the moment he'd died. He didn't tell her his real name or that he would have to go back to the spirit world again. Her mouth was open as she listened to what could only sound like a far-fetched tale.

"You expect me to believe that, do you?" she said. "Do you think I'm some sort of fool or that I was born yesterday? I just can't believe you'd waste my time like this here today. I hate you for it." She tried to leave, and John sprang to his feet in front of her. His face reddened, and he was clearly annoyed.

"Now you listen to me," he said, loudly, "I've told you the truth and I don't care if you believe it or not. I've passed through death with terrible regret. In fact, it was so bad, I was given a chance at a new life, which I took."

"Please stop," she shouted, putting her hands over her ears. John took them away.

"How can you prove this?" she said, loudly. He looked at the sky above him and the white wispy clouds moving quickly against the blue background as if he was searching for an answer.

"We all have angels and spirit guides. If you ask your guide for a sign to help you, believe it will happen. Don't tell me what the sign is. When you get, it tell me then, and if it's what you asked for maybe then you'll believe me." Caroline folded her arms in a petulant sort of way and looked away from John. After a few seconds, she turned around and faced him.

"Okay, I've asked, and if it doesn't happen, you'll have to tell me what's really going on. Goodbye." She walked off and John didn't try to stop her. He was now wondering again about the wisdom of staying on earth. He decided to call Rainbow to tell him he wanted to cross over, but Rainbow was not responding to John's thoughts. "Rainbow," he said in his mind, "I don't know why you're not answering me, but Caroline Finnegan is going to ask for a sign. It's important that she gets it. Please help her and help me. I don't know if I want to stay here, I have many doubts." John waited for a sign of some sort but there was nothing. He would just have to wait and ponder his new existence more.

Chapter 14

Later that evening, John was back home watching television. He wasn't taking it in and was thinking of his meeting earlier with Caroline. He stood up to make himself tea but discovered he'd run out. He put on his coat and headed to the village which was just around the corner from where he was staying.

He purchased tea and bread, paid the friendly shopkeeper, and left the small country shop. As he walked down the street, he heard somebody calling him. It was Ronna. She was sitting in her car on the other side of the road waving at him. John crossed over to where she was. "Hello," he said, looking surprised, "what brings you into Risk at seven o' clock on Saturday evening?"

"I'm meeting a friend for something to eat, and we're going for a drink afterwards. I see you're doing your grocery shopping," and she pointed to the groceries that he'd bought.

"Yeah," he said, "I always seem to run out just at the wrong time." There was silence for a few seconds and

Ronna fiddled with the steering wheel. "I better go," she said. "I'm meeting my friend at that restaurant down near the harbour. I'm supposed to be there by now."

"Okay, I'll bump into you on Monday no doubt," said John, smiling.

"I haven't forgotten about the feather," she said, suddenly. "I believed you when you said you didn't put it there, but I can't help feeling you know something about it." John put his hand on her arm and told her to have faith and to have a nice evening with her friend. He turned and walked away leaving her feeling unsatisfied.

Chapter 15

John got back to the yard just as it was starting to rain. He went up the steps, touched the horseshoe for luck and went inside. He was surprised to find Rainbow sitting at the table. He sat handling his long beard as usual and smiled at John. "Ah you're back, good, we can have a little chat now." John sat down and waited to hear what wise words the angel was going to come out with.

"I heard your thoughts yesterday," said Rainbow, "but I didn't want to rush in straight away with advice. So, you're thinking you might want to leave here and return to your real home, is that right?" John said he was considering it and that going back to the spirit world might be for the best. He said that he felt he was going around in circles.

"Don't let your thoughts or feelings run away with you," said Rainbow. "Caroline is going to get the sign she asked for because I will put it there. I can't say how she'll react, but she will know that nobody else knew about it. Maybe it will be a lesson in faith for her and a lesson in love for you."

"What do you mean a lesson in love?" asked John, sounding impatient.

"I mean don't jump yet. Don't give up. You know from your distant past that you tend to have a flair for running away at the wrong time. At least tell me you'll think about it." John was about to say something, but just then there was a knock at the door. Rainbow vanished from the chair and John opened the door to find Ronna standing outside.

"What are you doing here?" he asked. "I thought you were meeting your friend near the harbour."

"She felt sick and had to go home. As I was driving back past the yard, I said I'd call in. I hope that's okay or that you've no other plans. The small gate wasn't locked, don't worry I won't tell Joe." She followed this with a little laugh and looked over his shoulder into the room behind him. John felt happy, and his inward turmoil subsided. "It's lovely to see you, come in." Ronna walked in, looked around John's home, and thought it looked cosy despite its shabbiness.

"What do you usually do on Saturday evenings?" she asked, taking her cream-coloured trench coat off and sitting on the sofa.

"I might pop down to the pub or go for a solitary walk or sit here and watch telly, it depends on how I'm feeling at the time."

"What were you going to do tonight?" she asked, with a slight smile on her face. "Do you want to come out for a drink or something, obviously just as friends of course?"

"I'd like that," said John. He went to get his coat from the hook behind the door.

"Not immediately," said Ronna.

"Oh."

"Sit for a while and tell me about yourself." She patted the cushion beside her. John asked her if she'd like some tea.

"Let me make it," she said, jumping up suddenly, "I like doing things." John sat down and watched, as she made two mugs of steaming hot tea. She brought them over and sat next to him. They both stared in front of them for a few seconds. Ronna was the first to say something.

"You know, I still think you had some involvement with that feather. I don't believe you put it there, but I can't help feeling you know something about it."

"I didn't put it there," he replied, raising his voice slightly. "I'm happy for you that you've had a sign, just be glad to know there is somewhere after we die."

"Ah," she said, "now there you go again. You say that as if you know for certain, but nobody does, or do they? Do you know Mark? Do you know something I don't, tell me if you do?" John tapped the cup in his hand in a tense way. Ronna noticed and put her hand on his.

"It's all right," she said, "we can talk about other things." He didn't say anything and stood up to get more milk.

"It's nice here isn't it," said Ronna, now standing up and walking over to where John was pouring the milk. "I live at home with my family. It's nice there too. I live about four miles away. I have friends here in Risk and, as you know, I have a car. I was out of work for a few months following my brother's death, but now I'm back and in a new job. What's your story?" John lied to her by telling her how he had come to Risk to get away from the city. She listened with interest and then asked him how long he planned to stay in the job. "A few months, I suppose, depends on how long they want me for."

"What about after that?" she asked.

"I don't know yet," said John. "Why don't we give the questions a break and go and have that drink."

"I'd like that," said Ronna, smiling at him, and they got their coats and left.

Chapter 16

On Monday morning, John woke much earlier than usual. The room was dark and there wasn't a sound from the yard. He sat up and turned the small bedside lamp on. He fixed his eyes on the metal bar at the end of the bed and began to think about the previous Saturday night. He'd enjoyed Ronna's company, and they'd gone to a quiet bar near Loughsane. Nothing happened at the end of the night, but he got the feeling it could have if he'd encouraged it. She then drove him back to the yard and they said goodnight. Before she left him, Ronna said they would see each other at work on Monday morning, and then maybe talk about going out again sometime. John told her that he'd like that.

John now looked at the clock and saw that he still had a few hours to sleep before the alarm went off at seven. He turned the light off and lay down again.

Soon he was asleep and began to dream. He saw his family standing around his grave and putting flowers on the mound of clay. He stared at the grave and thought of himself lying under it. He could hear loud crying and it was a windy day. The wind carried the sound of the crying far away, and in the dream everybody for miles around could hear it. There was a very lonely feel to the scene.

Suddenly, the alarm clock went off and John slammed his hand down on the off button. The room was brighter now, and he was glad to find that he'd only been dreaming. He sat on the side of the bed for a few seconds to prepare himself for the new day. He yawned, stretched and put on his dressing gown. He went into the kitchen and put cereal into a bowl. He sat at the table and poured the milk while the kettle boiled. He then made some toast and had just finished eating it when his mobile phone rang. He answered it immediately.

"Mark, this is Caroline. I'm sorry for calling you so early and I would never have called you unless I felt I had to say something to you." She sounded agitated.

"Something like what?" he asked, scratching his head.

"That story you told me about the other day on the beach. I don't think I could ever believe it, but I got the sign I asked for. I had asked for a red handkerchief to appear in the bottom drawer of my dressing-table, and it did. Please don't say anything for a moment," she said, sensing he was going to interrupt. "It appears and I say again appears," she continued, "that you might be telling the truth about signs, but appearances are often deceptive. I don't know where it leaves us. What is your real name I wonder, or is all this some illusion you've caused to happen? I might be in touch, but I don't think it's very likely." John heard the line going dead. "Where indeed does it leave us?" he asked himself. He finished his breakfast in bad humour and went to work.

Chapter 17

The following day was fine, and Caroline found herself outside the lighthouse where her friend Clair lived. She knocked at the door and heard movement from within. The door opened and the actress palm reader stood dressed in her nightgown.

"Caroline, good to see you come in." Caroline came in and shut the door behind her. "Sorry if I got you out of bed, Clair, but I just had to talk to you."

"No, I was up early today, I'm just reading over my lines, and I felt too lazy to get dressed." They went into the round room where they'd been a few days ago with John and sat down.

"I've just made fresh coffee, let me get you a cup." Clair went off to the kitchen and Caroline thought of her last visit there.

"There we go," said Clair as she returned with the cup. She poured the coffee and sat back on a pile of cushions. "You look like you've got something on your mind, am I right?" Caroline looked at her. "Yeah, the other day when Mark was here, what was that all about?"

"Ah, the palm reading. It was the strangest reading I've ever done. Do you believe me? You don't think I'm a charlatan, do you?"

"No, of course not, I know your powers from coming to get my own palm read, and you've always been spot on in your readings," replied Caroline. She went to say something but hesitated and drank the coffee.

"What is it exactly you want to know?" said Clair.

"I want to know what exactly you saw in Mark's palm." Clair poured more coffee and munched on a biscuit. "I saw nothing, that's just it. There was nothing in the lines on his palm, it was as though he never existed. No history, no future nothing. I can't explain it. That's all I can say on the matter." Caroline looked disappointed.

"Is there something else?" asked Clair, noticing the look on her friend's face.

"Yes, there is," answered Caroline. "The other day after we left you, I pressed Mark on what this meant. I knew he was hiding something, and I wanted an answer. He said he couldn't give it to me at that time and we parted soon after. I couldn't get it out of my head, and I felt miserable. He contacted me and offered to meet me at the sand dunes with an explanation. I went to meet him."

"Oh my God, this I have to hear. What did he say?"

"You'll find this hard to believe," said Caroline, "but here goes. He told me he lived a life before this one, but under another name. He didn't tell me the name. He told me that he'd died, but that he'd been given a second chance at life. I didn't believe him of course and I was annoyed with him for wasting my time. He insisted it was true and told me that everybody has a spirit guide and to ask for a sign. I didn't believe it of course, but I liked Mark and so I asked for a sign in my mind. I got it." Clair was amazed at what she was hearing. "What are you going to do now?"

"I have got in touch with him and told him what happened, but that I still couldn't believe him, and that I did not want to be involved with someone who's clearly not telling the truth. That's how it stands now. What is he hiding? Is he mad?" Clair put her fingertips together.

"I really don't know how I can help you with this. Leave it for a while and observe him. Maybe some logical explanation will reveal itself. If he's not Mark, then who is he?"

"He wouldn't tell me what he was called before," said Caroline, "I don't like it, and I'll be keeping my distance."

"Let's finish our coffee, and I'll tell you about my part in the play. It'll be good to get this business with Mark out of your mind for a while." Clair reached for the script and showed it to Caroline.

"Yeah, you're right," said Caroline and she tried to dismiss the mysterious Mark from her thoughts.

Chapter 18

"Mark, come into the office for a minute." It was Joe Hammond's voice. John walked across the yard wondering if he was in some sort of trouble with the un-smiling foreman. He went in and closed the door behind him. "Is everything all right?" asked John, his voice sounding worried.

"Hold on, give me a minute," said Joe, as he searched through a drawer in the desk. John wondered what was going on. He didn't see Ronna.

"Ah, here it is," said Joe, pulling out a sheet of paper from under a file. "Just sign that will you and then you can go."

"What is it?"

"You've been given an extension to your employment here for a further five months. Do you want it or don't you? Sign that if you do." John took up the greasy pen that Joe had tossed across the desk to him and signed the name, Mark Foynes. He looked at it and wondered how he'd ever get used to writing it.

"That's all," said Joe, taking back the signed sheet of paper. "You can go now about your work."

"Is Ronna coming in today?" said John, wondering where she was.

"She'll be here later, her family are going to a memorial thing in the church for her brother. He died not too long ago. She'll be in at lunchtime. What are you intending to do today?"

"I was going to get rid of those weeds in the south field and then mend that broken window frame in the glasshouse beside the green gate." Joe grunted and said okay. John turned to leave.

"By the way, do you like working here?" asked Joe. John was bit startled by the question, especially from a man like Joe Hammond who wasn't big on people's feelings.

"Yeah, I've no problems with it," said John.

"What about Caroline Finnegan? I don't see her around much, what did you do to frighten her off?"

"Nothing," said John. "Anyway, that's my business," and as he left the office, he could hear Joe laughing behind him. He walked across the yard to the tractor and saw Clair Frawley standing beside it.

"Hello again," she said in her slow voice, "I'm on my way to rehearsals, and as I was passing, I thought I'd say hello."

"You're not here to read my palm again, are you?" said John, feeling uncomfortable. She smiled at him.

"No nothing like that. I was intrigued by our little chat the other day though. It's not possible for somebody to have nothing in the lines on their palm. I had a little visit from Caroline, and she told me the story you gave her about yourself. Maybe you should be a writer with an imagination like that."

"What I told Caroline is our business, nobody else's. She shouldn't have told you. It also happens to be true." Clair came closer to where he stood and whispered, "Don't hurt Caroline. She's a dear friend of mine and she doesn't need somebody with baggage coming into her life."

"Everybody has baggage, I'm sure you have too."

"Unlike you," Clair replied sharply, "I'm not an imposter. I am who I say I am. You on the other hand are running from something. My final word to you is this, don't hurt Caroline." John was about to say something, when suddenly Joe came out of the office.

"Are you still here, oh sorry Clair, I didn't see you there."

"I won't delay him any longer, Joe, we were just having a little chat. Bye for now," and she walked out the gate with a swagger.

"What did she want?" asked Joe.

"Nothing important," replied John.

"Well, go to the south field then and get that work done. You're not being paid to stand around here and chat." John didn't say anything and watched Joe marching back to the office.

Chapter 19

John climbed into the tractor and was to start it when his mobile phone started to ring. "Hello," he said, wondering who was calling him at that time.

"It's me, Caroline." John was surprised to hear from her and told her so. "How are you?" he asked in an impatient voice.

"I'm all right. I've been thinking more about what you said, and though I find it hard to believe, I can't explain getting that sign. I've decided it's all too weird for me and for that reason I don't feel I can meet with you ever again." John was silent.

"Hello, Mark, are you still there?" said Caroline, wondering what he'd got to say for himself.

"Yeah, sorry about that. I don't know what to say. I don't want anything to come between us. I understand how you must feel about all this, but it's happening to me, and I must live it out. I missed out the first time I lived, and I don't want it to happen again."

"Stop please," said Caroline, "I can't deal with this. I feel you're a nice person, but I can't get my head around this. I wanted to say also, that I'll have to be collecting stuff from the yard there and I don't want it to be awkward between us. I'd like if we could just do what we're supposed to and let there be no more talk between us. I'm sorry if that sounds cruel, but it's better that way."

"I understand," said John, "but what I told you is true."

"Feel free to meet someone else if you want, I will too. Your secret or fairy tale or whatever you'd call it, is safe with me." John didn't mention the conversation that he'd had earlier with Clair.

"Okay, well then, I'll try to avoid you when you call to the yard next time. Bye for now."

"Bye," she answered, and the line went dead. John looked at his mobile. "The phone is dead, just like me," he said quietly, and he stuffed it back into his pocket.

He started the tractor and drove off towards the south field. As he drove, a lot of thoughts were swimming around in his head. A car beeped at him, as the tractor had gone over the white line in the centre of the road.

"Watch where you're going, you could have caused an accident," shouted an angry driver from the car window. John looked blankly at him for a second and then turned away.

"If I crashed now, I wouldn't die or couldn't die," he said to himself. He laughed at the thought, but he didn't really think it was funny. He thought about the old saying, that life goes on after you're gone, but it felt odd to be still in it. "I died," he said to himself, "I'm still here, but I died." He pulled into the side of the road and turned off the engine. It was quiet, and he could hear the birds singing in the trees overhead. Suddenly, Emma's face appeared in the mirror of the tractor. She looked at him with a very direct gaze.

"Think about what you want to do," she said. "You know why you are here. Nobody ever gets this opportunity. I can tell you I've been a spirit guide a long time and I've never known anyone to get a chance like this before."

"You must admit," said John, addressing the mirror, "that it's a strange situation to be in. What is love, where is love?" Emma looked hard at him. "I lived, I worked, I found love. I died before my time following a kick from a horse. I was called from this life early, but not before I found love. You left this world before you found love. Now you have what's probably the first-time opportunity that anybody's ever had. A chance to come back here and find love." John looked down at the steering wheel and back again at Emma. She smiled at him.

"Think about it," she said in a matter-of-fact sort of way. "Now you've got a field to attend to, so you better go before you get sacked." Suddenly, she was gone, and John sat for a few minutes, much affected by her words.

The noise of a car whizzing by shook him out of his reverie. He started the engine again and drove off.

Chapter 20

John arrived back in the yard at lunchtime. He parked the tractor and noticed how quiet it was. He didn't check in with Joe, and instead went straight to his home at the top of the steps. He put the kettle on and took a chicken sandwich out of the fridge. While the kettle boiled, he sat down and read yesterday's newspaper. The kettle clicked off, and John made himself a pot of tea. He sat down again and tucked into the sandwich with relish. He looked over the headlines while enjoying his food. He had not closed the door properly, and he heard footsteps approaching. The door was slowly pushed back, and Ronna appeared on his threshold. She looked happy and was carrying the big feather in her hand.

"Hello there," she said, smiling. "Is it all right to come in?" John got up from his chair and threw the paper aside. "Of course, come in. I'm just having my lunch would you like a cup of tea?" She said she would, and he poured it into a cup. He put a packet of biscuits on the table and told Ronna to help herself. "There's nobody in the yard," she said. "They'll be back in few hours. Joe told me to tell you that you're to work with me in the office today."

"Yeah, I kind of thought I would be there today," he replied. "Is that the same feather?" he asked, looking at it in her hand. Ronna twirled it around. "This is an incredibly special feather. I'll never leave it out of my sight." She looked at John. He looked away and then back again a few seconds later. She looked down at the feather again and then back at him.

"What is it?" he asked.

"I think you know something about this feather, but I can't fathom what it is. I believe you when you say you didn't put it where I found it, but I just know you had something to do with it. Look me in the eye and tell me I'm wrong." He didn't answer and went on drinking his tea.

"I was in the church yesterday," said Ronna, "remembering my brother. I had lost all hope and faith when he died. Then for some reason after talking with you, I felt happy again. Then this feather found its way to me from Peter. Found its way into my drawer, imagine that."

"You know you've asked me about this before, why don't you just leave it and be happy that Peter is somewhere?" Ronna crossed to where he sat and kissed him, "What's troubling you, please tell me, I care about you?" she said. John held her tightly and whispered into her ear everything that had happened to him, and that how his name was really John Hughes and not Mark Foynes. He even told her the date of his death. It all just came out so easily. She didn't look up at him, but he felt her embrace getting stronger. He had not told Caroline his real name. Somehow it seemed right to tell Ronna. She exuded understanding and compassion.

"I believe you," she said, looking up with tears in her eyes. John thought there was something beautiful, almost simple about her reaction to his strange story. He chose not to tell her about the condition that the board had placed on him. He felt it wasn't the right time yet.

"I hope I don't get your name mixed up," she said. "God, what a strange story."

"Yes, I know. I'm Mark everywhere except when we're alone."

"Come on, John," she said, "we have work to do." And together, they walked down the narrow steps towards the office.

Chapter 21

Joe Hammond drove into the yard with a pile of wooden stakes intended for fencing, the old ones having fallen down in places, leaving gaps around the fields.

"Mark are you there?" he bellowed. John came out, "Yeah, I'm here working on that endless bundle of paper. Ronna's in there too, hard at it."

"Where's Dan?" said Joe, looking around.

"Here I am, Joe." And Dan appeared from around a corner.

"I want you and Mark to split this load. Put one half on the trailer and hook it up to the tractor. I want you both to make a start on the new fence. Dan, take Noel with you, and Mark, you take Willie." Dan wasn't looking forward to the work and he moved reluctantly to the van. Noel soon joined him, and they began the task of dividing the load. John and Willie joined in and soon the four men were unloading the heavy wooden stakes.

Joe went into the office and found Ronna working through the mountain of paperwork. She looked up when she heard the office door opening. "Ah, Joe, I'm hard at it here. Mark's been giving me a hand. He's particularly good at this."

"Yeah, well he's doing something else now, so you'll have to continue on your own. I have some calls to make so I'm going to use the inner office phone. If anyone calls or rings for me, tell them I'm not here." He went into the small office and closed the door loudly behind him. Ronna looked in the direction of the door and wondered if something was bothering him. "Maybe he's just being his usual horrible self," she said to herself, and turned her attention back to her never-ending work.

An hour later, Ronna heard a van driving into the yard. She got up and went out to see who it was. The men were gone to repair the fence and Caroline Finnegan was getting out of the van. Ronna was surprised to see her. She knew Caroline from the shop in the village, and had seen the van in the yard before, but apart from that, she'd never spoken to her. "I wasn't expecting you today," said Ronna. Joe Hammond didn't say anything about a collection. Caroline didn't answer straight away, and Ronna wondered why she was there.

"I'm not here to pick up supplies, in fact it's not work related," said Caroline, "I'm here to see you."

"Oh really," replied Ronna. "What do you want to see me about?" She sensed some friction between them. Caroline looked around the yard and asked if they could talk in the office.

"No," said Ronna, "Joe Hammond is in there." She looked towards the vegetable store and saw that it was unlocked. She pointed to the door. "We can talk in there." They went inside and Caroline suddenly turned on Ronna.

"You think you know Mark well, don't you?"

"We've got to know each other," said Ronna, feeling her face going red with anger. She sat down on a wooden crate and looked at Caroline in a dismissive way. Ronna sensed Caroline had come over on the attack and to Caroline it felt as though Ronna was going to defend Mark, as she had probably fallen for him.

"So, what do you want to talk about?" said Ronna.

"I'll tell you what," replied Caroline, raising her voice. "You've got feelings for Mark Foynes, haven't you? Don't bother answering. Things get around in a small place like this. I've seen you both from the shop window. I'm just telling you this for your own good. He's mad or else he's hiding something. He's probably running from the law."

"What are you talking about?" said Ronna. "Is this some sort of jealousy on your part? You're right, it is a small place around here and I've heard things too. You liked him once and still do I'd say. Don't bother trying to deny it." Caroline felt her temper rising within her and couldn't resist telling what she knew about John. "Do you know for instance," she said, "that he thinks he's an angel no, a lost soul walking the earth with a second chance to find love. He's clearly psychiatric." Caroline expected Ronna to jump up and defend Mark, but Ronna didn't reply for a minute. She stood up and looked into the yard. She then turned and looked at Caroline.

"You little fool, coming in here saying hurtful things. I know about Mark; he's told me it all, and I believe him. He's a good man and he deserves a second chance."

"Do you mean to tell me," said Caroline, "that you believe that tale that he's spun? Why is he doing it, ask yourself, because he's running from something." She walked towards the door.

"You want him, don't you, come on admit it?" said Ronna. Caroline turned and glared at her but didn't say anything.

"Well, you can't have him, and what's it all to you anyway?" said Ronna. Caroline left the store and slammed the door behind her. Ronna heard her hurrying across the yard and driving off. She went to the window and saw the back of the van as it passed through the gate. She stood looking at the gate for a moment and then looked up at the sky. Suddenly, she felt depressed. It was as if a black cloud had engulfed her. She turned her attention to the steps that led to John's room and thought about the strange situation that she was now a part of. "What if it is true and that he's disturbed in some way?" she asked herself. "No, he helped Peter to send that feather, I know he did. I've got to believe in him." She reached into her pocket and felt the feather. It made her smile.

Ronna went back to the office and resumed her work. She could hear Joe in the inner office, talking on the phone with someone about prices. She decided to forget her conversation with Caroline for the time being and busied herself. The door of the small inner office opened, and Joe put his head out.

"Did I hear Caroline Finnegan's voice?" he asked.

"Yes," said Ronna, "she was just here to check something with Mark, she was gone in a few minutes." Joe scratched his head. "I thought I heard loud voices, like arguing." And he looked over his glasses at Ronna.

"Never mind," he said, "but remember every sound carries in this yard. It's the way the place is built. If there's loud voices coming from anywhere, I can hear it." And he went back into his office. Ronna got up from the desk and opened the main office door. She stood for a few minutes thinking about what Caroline had said and wondering where it would end. She couldn't get their conversation out of her head. She knew one thing for sure, she was happy, happier than she had been for a long time. She knew that her happiness had come in an unusual way.

"But so what," she said to herself, "I like a bit of the unusual, always have." Ronna found herself looking forward to John coming back, and smiling, she closed the door again.

Chapter 22

It was later than usual before John got back from repairing the fence. He had dropped Willie off at the small bungalow where he lived. He then drove into the yard and turned off the engine. There was a disconcerting silence all around. He closed the gate to the yard and proceeded up the steps to his room. When he got inside, he turned the light on and stood with his back to the closed door for a minute. The place felt strange to him. He couldn't put his finger on what it was as nothing seemed out of place or disturbed.

Shortly afterwards, John was sitting over a fried egg and tea. He had the television on and was glancing at it every now and again, between bites. Many thoughts were racing through his head at the same time. He was thinking of his life as John Hughes and his family and all the things that had happened to him. Then he thought of what might have happened if he'd lived longer. He quickly told himself not to dwell on it and that his old life may not have brought anything good into it if he'd lived longer. He felt himself getting into a sad mood and tried to concentrate on the television programme. His mind soon started to drift again, and he thought of his life as Mark Foynes. The second chance, a chance at love, the strangeness of it all. Caroline came to mind and how she must have thought he was mad. Ronna's image passed before his eyes, and it was followed by a pleasant feeling. His mobile phone started to ring, and he stood up to get it from his jacket pocket; he never took it to the kitchen table with him.

"Hello," it was Ronna's voice on the other end. "What are you doing at the moment?" she asked. John thought she sounded happy, and it helped to lift his spirits.

"I'm having my tea and glancing at the telly. It must be telepathy; I was just thinking of you." Ronna gave a little laugh. "Are you in work tomorrow?" she asked. He said he was.

"I'm not," she said, "do you fancy going for a drive on Saturday?"

"I'd love that," said John, and he felt his heart beating faster. Since coming back from the dead, he was more aware of his heart. He thought about what Rainbow had said about it and his cause of death.

"Okay then," said Ronna. "When and where do you want to meet?" They arranged to meet outside Fairley's pub at 2pm.

"I'm looking forward to it," said Ronna and followed it with another small friendly laugh. "I'll have the car with me, maybe we can go out to Loughsane. There are nice walks there."

"Well, if you're looking forward to it, I'm really looking forward to it," said John, and they both said goodbye and hung up. He was feeling excited, happy, hopeful. Everything suddenly seemed lovely to him, the sky, the clouds, the air, his room. He felt an energy running through him, a power, life itself.

"Ah, do you think you're feeling it," said a voice behind him. Turning around, John saw Emma standing in front of him. He didn't answer her, and she looked straight into his eyes as she always did.

"It feels nice, doesn't it?" said Emma. She told him to sit down, and she sat beside him.

"If I'm starting to feel love, it's a nice feeling. If this feeling I have now, gets better, it will be wonderful. There's a condition and you being my spirit guide know what I'm talking about." He stopped and looked down at his hands.

"Continue please," said Emma. John looked up and met her direct gaze again.

"What happens if I do feel and continue to feel a strong connection with Ronna?" he asked. "What will happen to her when I have to go back? Where will it leave her? What of her happiness? She deserves it too and especially after the death of her brother. Maybe I shouldn't get too close to her." Emma laughed. "Who do you think you're kidding? If you're developing feelings for her, you just can't turn them off like a light switch. People have tried that before, but it never works. Wasn't it the deal that you would get a chance to taste love?"

"I know that," said John, "but where does it leave Ronna? What would it be like for her if I wasn't there anymore?" Emma put her hand on his shoulder and continued looking into his eyes. He could feel her reading his thoughts. It was as though she was walking around inside his head and looking into all the dark corners of his mind.

"This is about you and for you, remember that at all times," said Emma. "You met Rainbow, he told you what the board decided. Ronna will meet other men in the future. This whole arrangement has been to let you feel love. You were brought back from the grave and given a chance. Use it, feel it, love it." She smiled at him, took her hand off his shoulder and vanished. He looked at the empty place. He couldn't get the conversation out of his head.

"Emma's right, I know she is, but what about Ronna?" he asked himself. He went outside and stood at the door. He pictured Ronna's face in his mind and knew that he was indeed feeling love.

Chapter 23

John stood outside Fairley's pub on Saturday. At the appointed time, Ronna drove up. He hadn't seen her coming and she beeped the horn to get his attention. She lowered the window and told him to get in. He went around to the other side of the car and got in. They kissed, and there was a feeling of excitement and happiness in the car. They were both starting to feel deeply in love with each other. Ronna started the car again and they sped off towards Loughsane. John started thinking about the time when he'd gone there with Caroline and how wrong it all went. Ronna noticed his distraction.

"Hello," she said, jokingly. "Are you in there?"

"Oh sorry, sorry about that, I was just lost in thought there for a minute." He put his hand on her arm as if to re-assure her. She gave him a quick smile.

"You're not worried about anything are you?"

"No, I'm not worried."

"Good," said Ronna, "we'll soon be there, it's not far."

Ten minutes later, they were parking in the small carpark near the harbour. John released his seat belt and was about to get out, when suddenly Ronna asked him to wait.

"Are you all right?" he asked.

"Open the glove compartment," said Ronna. John reached down and opened the little black door. Inside, he saw the feather.

"You know all about the feather, don't you?" said Ronna. He took it up in his hand and twirled it around.

"Yes," he said, looking back at her, "I know about it being put in the desk. It did come from the other side. Your brother is happy now, he will watch over you when you need him." At this, Ronna threw her arms around John and kissed him hard. It was a long kiss, and John felt he was floating away. He didn't remember ever being kissed like this before.

"I better let you up for air," she said, giggling and released her arms from around him.

"Did you feel something during that kiss?" said John. Ronna said she felt something special.

"That's exactly what I felt," said John. "I felt love." Ronna lay her head on his shoulder. "It's lovely to hear you say that. Let's walk to the tower out there." The old Martello tower was close to the cliff edge and usually attracted visitors, but there was nobody else there that day. They locked the car and walked up the slope in the direction of the tower. John saw the lighthouse where he'd had his empty palm read but tried to ignore it. It was a bright day and they felt light, happy and contented. Ronna was feeling love and happiness, having John with her, and now believing her late brother was still with her. John was feeling love too, and he revelled in the joy of it. He felt a sweet, caring, happy feeling surrounding him.

They reached the grey ivy-clad tower and sat down on the tartan rug that Ronna had brought with her. Now and again, noisy seagulls flew overhead. Wispy clouds moved slowly across the blue sky. It was a nice place to be, and they liked having it to themselves.

"What are you thinking?" asked John. Ronna looked out at the sea and at the little harbour far below them, where the fishermen were busy unloading their catch.

"I'm not thinking of anything really," she replied. "It's just nice to be here with you. How about you?"

"I'm thinking that I'm falling in love with you but it's complicated. You know my story; you believe it and still you want to stay with me."

"Of course," she said, in an earnest voice. "I want you more than ever." He fiddled with the fringe at the edge of the rug and turned and looked at the Martello tower. "If I could always be here with you like that tower, I'd be happy, but if we continue like this and if our love grows stronger, I will have to go back. That was the condition on which I agreed. It was the only reason that I was able to come back to earth." Ronna felt tears in her eyes and tried to hold them back. "I didn't know there was a limit on your time here," she said. "Maybe I can go back with you, or maybe they'll leave us alone."

"I don't think it'll be like that. I was given a special chance to find love, but with a stipulation. I found you and at this present moment I love you and I'm here with you now." He pulled her to him.

"I love you too," said Ronna, "yes we are here now just you and I and that's all that counts," and she kissed him, softly. At that moment, he felt joy, but just that bit closer to his new home in the spirit world.

Chapter 24

Several weeks went by and it was now common knowledge around the yard, and the town that Ronna and John (or Mark, as he was known to everybody), were an item. Caroline saw them from time-to-time walking past the wide shop window, hand in hand. She told herself she didn't miss Mark and that his secret dream world was not for her. She did, however, feel envious of their apparent happiness, and it caused her to wonder sometimes about hers, when she was alone with her thoughts. John continued to work for Phil Clarke and for now he was happy. When not working together on the paperwork, John would come back from a morning's work in the fields at lunch hour and find Ronna waiting for him either in the office or in his small kitchen. His new life had become a contented one. He didn't think of his family much anymore, and his focus was entirely on Ronna. He hadn't heard from Rainbow or Emma for several weeks and hoped he wouldn't for a long time to come. Life continued that way and his love for Ronna deepened. They usually went out once or twice during the week and at the weekends. He now felt it was impossible for him to be happy without her. Ronna felt the connection with her dead brother was becoming more natural through John. This, she felt was essential in keeping her from falling into terrible grief.

One day while Caroline was getting ready to go to Clarke's yard for vegetables, her father came in and asked her to hold on for a few minutes before going. She looked surprised and wondered what he was going to say.

"You're a bit off these days, am I right?" he asked. Caroline wondered where this was going.

"I'm okay, Dad, really I am. I know you heard something about me and Mark Foynes being friends and then not being, but it's not troubling me too much." Jack looked at her with a serious look on his face. She knew something was coming, as this was what he always did when he was going to say something that she didn't want to hear.

"I don't want you to be upset. You can do better than him. He just drifted here to Risk, got a job and may I add not in the usual way. Maybe he's done nothing wrong, but I've seen the way you watch him and that other girl when they pass the window." Caroline started to feel emotional, she couldn't believe the effect that her father words were having on her. She still did have feelings for John but felt she couldn't accept his lies. She thought about the stupid childish story that he'd told her. Her mind wandered back to the first time they'd met and how happy she'd felt. She thought of the drive to Loughsane and afterwards when it had all gone wrong.

"Hello, Caroline, come back to me." Her father was calling her back to the present moment. His voice intruded into her thoughts, and she felt annoyed by the sound of it.

"Are you still with me?" he asked.

"It's okay, Dad, yes I'm still with you."

"I think I lost you there for a minute. Look, all I'm saying is don't get too upset over Mark Foynes." Caroline was silent for a moment and without thinking said, "he said he worked in Whelehan's in town, you know the big food place, but I since found out he didn't. I liked him, Dad, I still do, but he's hiding something, and I feel insulted and hurt by him."

"I wonder why he said that if it wasn't true," said Jack Finnegan. "Did you ask him about it?" Caroline wasn't expecting her father to say that, and she was a bit taken off her guard.

"Well," said her father, "did you? maybe there's some good reason for it, though to tell you the truth, I can't imagine what it is."

"He told me some silly story about himself, but it's so stupid I'm not going to repeat it. I don't know what's going on with him." Ronna's father didn't say anything and stood looking over her shoulder.

"Dad are you still there?" Jack was trying to figure out what exactly was going on.

"You seemed to drift of too. What do you make of it?" asked Caroline.

"It looks to me like he might be hiding something as you say. Maybe he's broken the law. I might ask my friend at the Garda station to keep an eye on him or find out more about him." Caroline started to regret saying anything, but it just seemed to roll so easily off her tongue. Although she was annoyed with John, she didn't want to get him into trouble. "Don't do anything hasty, Dad, please promise me you won't."

"Don't worry," he said, "I'll be very discreet, don't you be worrying about it. Now you better go to Clarke's and collect those vegetables." He gave her nose a gentle pinch that made her smile and walked back towards the shop. Caroline was troubled and felt she'd said too much.

"What now?" she asked herself. Though Mark Foynes had a strange story to tell, she couldn't help feeing strange herself. Everything around her seemed to feel peculiar; she couldn't put her finger on it. It felt as if her life was changing and yet it wasn't. She was annoyed with Mark and yet she was happy to know him. "I'm sure that's not his real name," she told herself. "I suppose everything about him is false."

She jumped into the van and started the engine. She drove the short distance down the main street and turned in the direction of Clarke's yard, wondering if she'd meet the mystery man and what she'd say to him if she did.

Chapter 25

Caroline drove into the yard and saw Dan coming towards her. He was carrying a bunch of Keys on a large keyring, making him look like a jailer. He waved to her. "Hello Caroline, we haven't seen you here for a while, your father usually picks up the stuff now. How are you?"

"I'm fine," she replied, getting out of the van. "Is Mark around to help me load up?"

"No, he's away now, but he'll be back later. I've to help you." Dan went to the door of the store and opened the lock. Caroline got back into the van and reversed it towards the store. She got out again and proceeded to load the produce with Dan.

"We've missed you coming into the yard," said Dan. "It's nice to have you back again. Did you have some disagreement with Mark?" Caroline gave him a hard look but then seemed to calm down quickly.

"It's not really any of your business, but yes we did."

"I thought so," said Dan, "I knew you liked each other. What happened?"

"Look Dan, I don't want to offend you, but it's my business. Sometimes we just don't know where we stand with people who are supposed to like us, anyway, let's just get the job done." Dan grunted and the conversation between them ceased.

"That's the lot," said Dan, when they'd finished loading, "Can I just get you to sign for them." She took the pencil he gave her and signed her name. "Thanks, Dan, I'm not going to hang around, I've got things to do." He nodded to her, and she got into the van and started the engine. Just as she was driving out the gate, John came walking through. They both had an uncomfortable feeling. Caroline nodded to him but didn't stop. He nodded back. He thought she was going to stop and turned to talk to her, but she drove on.

She didn't drive straight home but pulled in a short distance from the yard. It was an obscure enough spot for her not to be seen. She started to go over everything in her head and the crazy story that Mark had told her about coming back from the dead. She pulled out her mobile phone and called Sheila.

"Hello," answered Sheila.

"Hello, Sheila, it's me, I'm not sure why I called you."

"Ah, hiya, is everything all right? You sound a bit out of sorts or something." There was silence down the other end of the phone for a few seconds.

"I thought I'd got Mark Foynes out of my head," said Caroline, "but when I saw him for a second today, I felt a pull. Is he a crook do you think?"

"Why has he not told you the truth about himself? That's what you said to me on the phone the other night. He's hiding something for definite. Then he goes and gives you a lot of rubbish about being dead and living again. Come on, forget him, who needs someone like that." Caroline wondered if she'd done right in telling Sheila all that she knew.

"I know I know," said Caroline, "but somehow, I feel he's a good person. He's going around with the girl who works in the office. She knows something about him, of that, I'm sure. Please don't tell anybody about this conversation."

"No, not a word. Can you believe that fool in the office is taken in by him?" There was silence down the phone.

"Hello, Sheila, are you still there," said Caroline, fearing they'd been cut off.

"Yeah, I'm still here. Maybe don't do anything for the moment or get impatient. We'll watch him. We'll soon suss out what's happening. He must have come from somewhere."

"You're right," said Caroline, "we'll work together. If he's got nothing bad to hide, then I might like to be with him again. We'll find out."

"What about the girl in the office, Ronna, I think her name is?"

"Oh, she'll soon get sick of his secrets, she won't stay around. I can't believe she's standing by him," said Caroline with a sound of irritation in her voice. They said they'd meet up in a few days and hung up. When Caroline came off the phone, she suddenly didn't feel so sure of anything anymore which caused her to stare at a nearby field for what seemed like ages. It was five minutes before she broke from her stupor and drove off again.

Chapter 26

Time continued to pass by, and John worked hard on the land, in the yard and with Ronna on getting the paperwork sorted. Their relationship flourished, and John learned it was possible to love again. He thought of his early days with Clara and how she had been a huge loss in his life. He tried to imagine himself back then, but it all seemed so long ago now. He had been careful in the years after she'd gone, so careful in fact that it came across as being cold, stinting and aloof. The closeness and love between him and Clara had been damaged unnecessarily. It had made him bitter, sullen, envious and resentful. He had become confused at the time and had grown increasingly discontented. John wondered how with such bitterness he brought into his life that he could be given a second chance. "People are nice, people do really love. There's no need to be fearful," he said to himself over and over.

A few days later, John was in a restaurant with Ronna. They were having a sumptuous dessert and were oblivious to everything around them. The love between them was growing more. Sometimes John would pinch himself to see if it was all some fantasy. For Ronna, she felt the same and she carried the feather everywhere with her to remind herself that it was real.

Ronna felt that she loved John and through him she would always have contact with her dead brother. She had accepted John's story of what had happened to him but didn't think about it too much. She had fallen for him completely. He was everything to her now.

They left the restaurant and walked out to the carpark which was at the back of the building. Ronna opened the car and they both got in. John was putting on his seatbelt when she turned to him and said, "Don't put your belt on yet, can we sit here for a few minutes and talk?"

"Yeah, that's okay with me," said John. Ronna took the feather from her handbag and looked at it and then at John. She smiled, and he kissed her. He felt happy and Ronna was happy too.

"I know you told me the story about your getting a second chance and I believe you, but where does it leave us in the future? Have you told me everything?" John looked away and she put her hand on his cheek. "Look at me," she said, in a gentle voice. He turned his head and looked at her in a loving way. Just at that moment the sun came out and John felt his heartbeat quicken.

"Well," she said, smiling, "are you going to talk to me?"

"You know my real name, my story etc., and about my having to go back."

"Oh yes, that," said Ronna, her expression becoming serious.

John hesitated and then said, "I really do have to go back at some stage."

"What do you mean go back, tell me, John, do you mean you will die again?" He could hear anguish in her voice. He knew she would feel worse grief when she turned, and he was no longer there. Ronna thought of her brother Peter and how he could never come back to her. She would never see him until she met him someday somewhere in another world. John had helped her with the feather, and it meant so much to her in lonely moments. Now John would be leaving her, and she hated it. Her upset grew to desperation.

"No," she said loudly, "I want you here with me always. Now that we've met, I can't be without you."

"I feel like that too of course," said John, "but that's not the way it works. When I was last on earth, I led a mean life and yet I was given this chance to find and taste love. I found it when I found you."

"Then we keep it and hold on to each other," she said back with a cry in her voice. John hugged Ronna and pressed her close to him. "The condition was that after I found love and had some truly happy moments, then I would have to return."

"What about me?" said Ronna, her voice rising again. John felt lost for words. He didn't know how to answer her.

"If you're going, I'm going with you," said Ronna.

"No, I mean how, what are you saying?"

"I don't know yet," she answered, "I only know I'm not staying here without you." John held her hand and looked downward.

"Have you heard from Rainbow?" asked Ronna.

"No, but I'm sure I will. I know the way I'm feeling about you and if it continues, then it's only a matter of time before I hear from him." Ronna suddenly kissed him and smiled.

"Why are you smiling?" said John. She laughed and ran her fingers through her hair.

"I want you not to worry and for us to continue as we are. When Rainbow thinks you've had long enough, you will say that you wish to apply to the board for another deal."

"I don't think that's the way it's done," said John, "but we'll continue as we are until I hear from him."

"It's a deal," said Ronna and they shook hands.

Chapter 27

The days flew by, and John was busier than ever. Occasionally Caroline came to collect the produce form Clarke's yard. Sometimes she would load up the van with the help of John. They wouldn't have much conversation when doing this, but when they did, it was usually a strained attempt at general chat. There was, however, an atmosphere or feeling between them. John felt it but he didn't want it. He now loved Ronna. Caroline felt it too, but she didn't try hard to fight it. She saw something in John, something she wanted to touch. It was as if she wanted to make him feel he could be honest with her and put some light into his empty eyes. Lately though, she was beginning to see happiness in them, a happiness that he had found with Ronna Smyth. She thought about his crazy story, but recently she had begun to care less about it. She still didn't believe it of course, but it mattered less what the truth was. She was slowly feeling more and more attracted to him.

One day while working in the office together, Ronna turned towards John and asked him if he loved her.

"Yes," he replied. "Of course I do, and you?"

"Me too." And they kissed. Just at that moment, Joe walked in and almost saw them kissing.

"Where are we at with these invoices and the rest?" asked Joe, clearing his throat.

"We're way on top of it now," replied Ronna. "Another few weeks should have it all in order. There's been an awful lot of work in it. Mark here has been a huge help." And she smiled at John as she spoke. Joe, like everyone else knew there was something between them, but he didn't care. He had no major interest in other people. He just wanted the work done and as quickly as possible.

Later that day after they'd finished work, Ronna had a cup of tea with John before driving home. "Do you really love me?" she asked. He looked at her and laughed.

"Yes, I do, you know I do, but what are we do about it?"

"What do you mean, what do people do who love each other?" Her face grew serious, and she didn't like his question.

"You know the condition for me being allowed to stay here. If we have a love for each other, then it's only a matter of time when I'll be called back." Ronna was of course aware of this, but she had been pushing it out of her mind. She didn't want to believe it. "If that happens,

I want you to talk to Rainbow. I want him to give us more time or failing that, I'm going with you."

"No, it's not meant to be like that. You must live your life. That is not how it goes."

"I'm sure," she said with tears appearing in her eyes, "that what happened to you wasn't meant to be either, but it did." John held her in his arms and they both said nothing more for a few moments. Suddenly, he broke the silence. "I can feel them calling me back. They know I have found love with you. They know I have at last experienced the feeling long enough to recognise it. I knew love early in life, but I grew afraid, remote, too deep and lost that love forever. You have brought the feeling back to me."

"What will you do?" asked Ronna, resting her hand on his lap.

"I'll talk to Rainbow and see what he has to say. I'll ask him what my options are."

"Thank you," said Ronna, kissing him. "Can I be there with you when you do?" John smiled and pushed back a strand of hair from her forehead. "No, you wouldn't see or hear anything. You have not passed through death yet. Don't worry I'll let you know what happens."

"Okay then. I know it'll be all okay." And Ronna embraced him tightly.

Chapter 28

Later that night, John made his way to the beach. It was dark and cold, and he sat in the sand dunes. The noise of the tide crashing in front of him, and the silence of the dunes helped him to concentrate. Between them they created a forlorn atmosphere. He immediately thought of Rainbow, and soon the colourful angel appeared in front of him.

"I know why you're here," said John. Rainbow sat down beside him.

"Yes, I'm sure my being here doesn't come as a surprise to you. I laid it out very plainly for you when we first met. I was going to be calling on you in the next few days."

"It's been a success," said John, starting to feel sad. "I met two women and I think they both felt love for me. One woman let me go, not because she didn't want me, but because she found my story insulting to her intelligence."

"Ah yes," said Rainbow, "I wondered if it was wise to tell Caroline, but then again look how Ronna reacted to your story." John felt the cold night air on the back of his neck and shivered. "I don't want to leave here. I feel I've found my true home. Ronna needs me too. She feels close to her dead brother through me and a certain feather. Can I stay?" he asked, with a sound of desperation in his voice. Rainbow looked at him with sadness. "I'm afraid I can't see that happening."

"I'm sure it's never happened before that somebody died and was let live again to experience love, so why not? Anything is possible with you, isn't it?"

"Can you be quiet for a moment," said Rainbow. John nodded his head. He watched as a glow seemed to surround the angel. The glow turned into a strong white light, and he couldn't look at Rainbow without feeling pain in his eyes.

Suddenly, the light vanished, and Rainbow looked at John. "You will have to plead your case with the board. They will let me know when, and I will come for you at the appointed time. It might even be as soon as tomorrow. Good luck, my friend." John was about to ask him for more details, but Rainbow quickly vanished.

"There may be hope, there may be hope," John repeated over and over, and he left the beach, feeling downcast. As he walked up the narrow sandy lane, he couldn't stop thinking about death, and what happens to a person's spirit afterwards.

He emerged from the lane and passed a small caravan site on his left that he hadn't noticed before. He found himself thinking about the families who holidayed there over the years. John hoped the children of these families would be happy in later life and that they would go the right way. He had an urge to knock on all the doors and tell him them how important it was to truly love, to be honest, be themselves and not pretend about anything. He wanted to show them how fear had no place in their lives, no matter where it came from. "If it's coming from within yourselves," he said to himself, "banish it now. If it's coming from somebody in your life, someone close to you or not, then get away from them. If it's harsh and brutal or subtle and sneaky, reject it now and genuinely love. Never be bitter, nasty, or resentful. Never let yourselves be humiliated by anybody no matter who it is, and never humiliate others. Never hurt anyone in any way. When real love comes to you, embrace it. Only this way, can light shine from your eyes. Don't pretend to be happy about your life if you're not. Never try to fool yourself. You will all die one day, that's for sure and then it's too late to change anything. Love and be loved, but only if it's true love, not some conditional changeable thing that only results in resentment, disappointment and disillusion." He felt he was understanding life at last and seeing it as it should be. At once, a memory came back to him. It was something that happened not long after he'd met Clara. He had felt crushed and heart-broken by things somebody had said to him in private on several occasions. He had mistakenly admired and looked up to this person, but they shattered him with their words and deeds. He now thought about how they had damaged him and caused him to withdraw and veer off his true course in life.

"Yes," John said to himself, feeling enlightened and liberated, "that was it. It threw me completely. I was very upset, but I began to believe it and it took root in my soul and mind. It affected my self-worth and my relationship with Clara. I should have told her; she would have helped me. She was always kind and understanding. I became withdrawn, resentful, hopeless, bitter, mean and cruel. It made me feel useless, angry and horrible. The angels know this and have left it to me to discover again. It's all part of the process, I know it is." He sat down on a small grassy mound nearby, took a long deep breath and exhaled slowly. The moon appeared for a brief moment and then went back behind the clouds. He imagined it was saying thank you for his truthful words, and then going back to sleep again.

After staying sitting for a short time, John got up and walked in the direction of his little home behind the red door.

Chapter 29

Three days passed since John's encounter on the beach with Rainbow. Ronna was still working hard in the office, continuing to put some order on the endless mountain of invoices, dockets and bills. She was placing everything in cardboard files alphabetically and in date order and inputting them on the computer also. John hadn't been working with her for a week as he had a lot to do on the land and in the glasshouses. Ronna would see him sometimes through the window of the office driving or walking into the yard. When nobody was around, she would knock on the glass to get his attention. He would always wave back and smile. To anyone who could have seen them at these times, there could be no questioning the love and closeness that had developed between them. Ronna liked to have her lunch with John in his small home. They laughed and talked a lot when they were together. She was easy to be with and had the effect of making him feel good about himself.

On the night of the third day after meeting Rainbow, John was sitting on the sofa looking at his mobile phone, when suddenly he felt someone standing behind him. Turning around, he saw three figures in white robes with wide red ribbons around their waists. He felt frightened, as they radiated a powerful force.

"Stay where you are," said one of the men in a voice that had an echoing sound. There were two men and a woman. The men had white beards and the white garments they wore, were shining brightly. The woman, also clad in dazzling white, had raven black hair tied back. They walked around to face John.

"John, you have come to our attention again. Rainbow tells us you want to stay here, that you have let love into your life and heart at last, is that true?" asked one of the men.

"Yes," answered John, "Rainbow said I would have to plead my case with the board. I'm waiting to be called to meet them." The woman smiled.

"We are the board. We thought you might talk easier here. You will have to tell us why you should or could stay on earth any longer. You know the agreement and have already been given a chance that nobody ever gets."

The angelic board now sat opposite him, smiling with the most amazing rays of light coming from their eyes. Despite the loving atmosphere, John felt afraid, and that he was on trial. It was not as if he was in court fighting for his freedom, but he felt his new happiness was at stake. He had found love in the strangest way. He had been given a chance to come back from the silence of death and find what he had mistakenly expelled from his young life the first time around. He started to feel nervous, and his hands shook uncontrollably. The woman looked at him with an intense gaze. "There's no need to feel frightened, we're not out to get you, John." John folded his arms to try and conceal the shaking. Then one of the men spoke, his voice sounded musical. "You would like to stay longer in this little town of Risk with a certain lady, isn't that so?"

"Yes, that's right," replied John, with a tremble in his voice.

"Let me introduce us to show you are among friends," said the other man. "I am Jansa, this is Feela," pointing to the woman, "and the other is Plaso. We are angels and have never lived the human life. Our business, however, is human life, and we guide and help when we are allowed to."

John sat up straighter on hearing this and said, "Can I ask you what you mean by saying when you are allowed to? I would have thought angels didn't need anyone's permission."

"We cannot force anybody to do something if they're not prepared to do it," said Plaso. "We can guide and send advice to people's souls; we connect in that way. Everybody has the gift of freewill. If they choose not to go the right way, that is their choice." John began to feel even more nervous.

"What happens to people like that?" he asked, his voice quivering. Feela spoke this time.

"When they die, they will spend longer in the life reviewing process before they can enter the garden of love. They must fully understand the mistakes they made and atone. When they're ready, they will move on. Everyone goes through the life review process as you already know. Depending on the life you led here on earth will determine how long you have to stay in the process."

"The main question at the moment is if you should be let stay here for longer, now that you feel you have found love," said Jansa. They sat there smiling and looking at John with an even stronger gaze. Anybody else would have said that their lives were in the hands of these three angels. John couldn't say that as he'd already lived his life. He wanted to live his pretend life for a bit longer if he could. He had indeed been given the chance to find love, and it had worked.

"You're gone quiet on us," said Feela. "You were told clearly by Rainbow what the condition was. Why should it now be changed?"

"Yes, I know the agreement that was made, but what about Ronna?" he replied. "Won't she be very upset if I'm just suddenly gone?"

"Yes, she will," said Plaso, "but it's not her life that we are now dealing with. She must make her own journey and she will receive guidance. Our concern is you and not Ronna." John started to feel upset and wondered again if he had done the right thing by coming back to the world.

"It was the right thing," said Feela, reading his mind, "but we must deal with this now. We have lots and lots of people who need our help and who will never have the chance that you had." John was afraid to ask the next question but ask he did. "Has a decision already been made?" They sat there and didn't speak for some seconds. Suddenly, Rainbow and Emma were standing on either side of John, and he felt their hands on his shoulders.

"Yes," said Jansa, "it has been decided that you will be given two more weeks to enjoy your new-found love." John felt tears in his eyes.

"What am I to tell Ronna?" he asked in a pleading voice. Her happy face appeared in his mind's eye. He could only imagine how she would feel at this news.

"You will tell her nothing," said Feela. "She will be upset of course when you leave here, but she is young and will meet others. Her guide will be watching out for her. Think clearly, ask yourself how long could this really go on for? People do not come back from death and live again. You were given a unique opportunity and you took it. You tasted love and you were happy, but it couldn't continue like that."

"But how do I tell her nothing? Imagine the grief she will feel," said John, his voice breaking.

"You will write her a letter," said Plaso. "Rainbow will put it in the drawer in the desk where she keeps her bag when she comes to work. She will also find a large feather. It will be a sign from you, we can make all this happen." John looked at the floor and was quiet for some moments. His mind was racing, and he found it maddening. He looked back at the angels and wondered if there was another way around his situation. They read his thoughts.

"No, John," said Feela, "there is no other way. You will spend the next two weeks enjoying the love between you both. We are aware that you find this hard, but really, it must be this way. You found love and when Rainbow comes to bring you to your new home, you will find that your life review process will be swift."

"Why will it be swift?" asked John.

"Because," said Plaso, "you have opened your heart to real love again. You feel it and you know what it is to lose it. If it were decided to leave you here for many more years to come, you would never again be hard, cynical, mean, cruel or even unhappy. You took the wrong road in life, but it wasn't your fault. It was, however, your choice to stay on that road and that was the mistake you needed to learn from. By having this one-off chance, you have learned to love and feel again." John couldn't think of anything more to say. It had all been put to him plainly, but there was still the question of Ronna.

"We must leave now," said Jansa, "other souls need us, and we have much work to do. You know what you have to do. You found what you came back for, and it has all been a remarkable success." Suddenly, the three angels started to shine even more with an incredible radiant light, and in an instant, they were gone. Rainbow was gone too and only Emma stood beside John. She smiled and placed her hand on his arm. "It will be all right, don't worry. Write your letter soon and when Rainbow comes for you, he will place it with a feather in the drawer. No locks or keys can stop him." John smiled back at her with tears in his eyes. Suddenly, she too was gone, and he now looked at the empty space where they had all been.

He went out to his front door and stood looking up at the stars. It made him think about heaven. He looked down at the yard and all the work that was waiting for him the next day. His eye caught the little window of the office, and he imagined Ronna knocking on the glass to catch his attention. "I do love her," he said to himself, "but I suppose she will find love with another in the future. The angels are right of course, but that still doesn't make it any easier. I'll write her that letter in a few days, but in the meantime, I will love her dearly."

Chapter 30

The next morning, John came down to open up the yard. When he opened the big wooden gate, Jack Finnegan was standing outside.

"Can I help you?" asked John.

"That depends on if you can tell me what you want, who you are, and why you have upset my daughter?"

"What is this?" asked John. Jack drew nearer to him with an angry face. "Where did you come from? There's something suspicious about you. I have friends in the guards, and I might just ask them to look in on you."

"I've done nothing wrong," said John, "so get lost and don't be annoying me."

"I'm going to be watching you, and if I get as much as a hint that you've been up to no good, I'm coming back with those friends of mine." After saying this in a snarling way, Jack got back into his van and drove off.

John went into the office and started laying out the paperwork for Ronna. He wondered what Caroline had said to her father. He looked at the drawer where Ronna kept her bag. He thought of what Emma had said about how no lock or key would stop Rainbow putting the letter and feather there. John heard someone driving into the yard. He went to the window and saw Ronna pulling up. He waved to her, and she waved back. He thought how lovely and happy she looked just at that moment. She came into the office and kissed him.

"Good morning," she said, in her usual cheerful way, "how are you on this lovely morning?"

"All the better for seeing you. I think I'm working in the far field today. Would you fancy coming out later, maybe Fairley's for a drink?"

"It's a date," replied Ronna, "but I better get to work on these. Will we meet at eight, I can pick you up from here?"

"Sounds good, I'll be here waiting," and he kissed her. As he was leaving the office, he looked again at the drawer.

"What is it?" asked Ronna.

"What's what, how do you mean?"

"You were looking at the drawer, don't tell me you saw a spider or something."

John laughed. "No, I was just daydreaming. See you there at eight." And he left the office. He met Joe, who was coming into the yard.

"I'm doing the far field today," said John.

"Right," said the grumpy foreman, "you better get going then." John climbed into the tractor and drove off.

Twenty minutes later, he pulled into the wide field and turned off the engine. Suddenly, Rainbow was standing in front of the tractor. John got out and walked over to him. "It's not time yet, is it?" he asked.

"Not yet," said Rainbow, "but you should be giving thought to writing that letter. I know you're going out tonight with Ronna, but I would be thinking about what you're going to write."

"I will, I will, there's no need to remind me." And John felt himself getting annoyed.

"Good," said Rainbow and he vanished. John turned to get back into the tractor and saw Jack Finnegan looking at him strangely from between the surrounding trees. *He'll surely think I'm mad, talking to myself,* thought John. He stared back and Finnegan looked away and hurried off. John started the engine and drove to a corner in the field. He got out and proceeded to clear a pile of old material that had been left there from a previous job. He lifted a large rotting plank and spotted a small dead bird. He picked it up and examined it closely. He couldn't see any injuries and wondered how it had died. He thought of his own dead body and compared it to the bird's.

"Perhaps you died from heart trouble," he said, feeling the lifeless feathers. "Just like me, no signs on the outside, but inside, a troubled ticker. I wonder did you have a loved one or what was your life like? I don't suppose you'll be given a chance to come back, maybe you don't need to." He took a spade from the trailer attached to the tractor and began to dig a small grave for the deceased bird.

When he had gone down about a foot, he took the lifeless creature and placed it gently in the ground. He looked at it and then imagined himself lying in his own grave. "Rest in peace," he said quietly, and covered the grave in.

Chapter 31

Three days later, John returned to his home in the yard after spending the evening with Ronna. They had gone to the local cinema and then for a drink afterwards. She had asked him if there had been any developments. He told her that he had been given an extension, but that he didn't know for how long. Ronna was happy that he had more time but was concerned about how long it might be for. John felt bad not telling her the time allotted to him, but he just couldn't do it. He didn't want her counting the days.

Later, he sat at his kitchen table with pen and paper before him and decided it was time to write his farewell letter. He took up the pen and, with an aching heart wrote.

Hi Ronna,

I'm afraid the time has come for me to say goodbye to you. I know this is going to hurt you very much, but I couldn't tell you about the little bit of extra time I was given. I don't think you or I would have been able for that scene.

As you know I was given a second chance to live again in order to find love. I found it with you. The time we have spent together has been the best time in my life, or should I say my second life. I found myself having feelings that I thought were dead inside me, feelings that I thought I would never have again. I had become sour, mean, hostile and afraid. I now know what caused me to become that way, but it all disappeared soon after I met you. You were a ray of sunshine in my darkness.

When I died, I was in my mid-forties and I did not look like who you got to know. I, as you know, was given the name Mark Foynes, but as you also know my real name was John, John Hughes. I died from heart trouble. It was as Mark Foynes that I really started to live the way I should have. It was because of you that I began to love again.

It is however, a very unnatural position to be in and one that couldn't go on much longer. I have lived my life, seen the errors of my ways through my new life, and must now make my journey from here.

I will never forget you and perhaps in many years to come, we will meet again. I have no doubt your brother will be there too.

Please try to love again and live your life in a happy way. I will try to send you a sign.

Yours always,

I love you,

John (Mark)

When he'd finished writing the letter, he got up from the table and went out to the sitting room to get an envelope. Rainbow was sitting on the sofa. He looked at John and handed him an envelope. John took it from him with nervous hands and put the folded letter inside. He sealed it and handed it back to Rainbow. The angel smiled.

"I will see that it gets to where Ronna will find it and a large feather too. I think she likes feathers very much."

"I calculate," said John, "that my time is up next Saturday morning. When exactly will you come or will it be you?" he asked, starting to feel afraid.

"Yes, it will be me," replied Rainbow. "I will be here at fifteen minutes past midnight on Friday night to take you to your new home. On Monday morning, Ronna will find the letter along with the feather. After you see her on Friday, she will be away for the weekend. Your number will disappear from her phone, and she will not be able to contact you. A message will be left on Joe's office phone saying you had to go away. I will put it there in your voice. He will not care much. Joe has a few life lessons to learn too when it comes to people's feelings."

"Will Emma be coming back?" asked John. He had thought her kind and would have liked to see her again.

"No," replied Rainbow, "she was your guide while you lived on earth. You will not see her anymore as you are now moving on." John sat down and rubbed his face.

"I suppose that's that then. Well until early on Saturday morning."

"Yes, until then," said Rainbow and he vanished with the letter.

Chapter 32

The remaining days passed quickly and life for John and Ronna continued happily along in each other's company. They had arranged to get Friday off and spent the day together. Ronna had no idea she was seeing John for the last time. He felt tearful at times but tried hard not to show it.

They started their day with a walk to the old Martello tower at Loughsane. It was chilly, and as they walked, they snuggled together from the cold.

"I won't be around this weekend," said Ronna, stopping "I'm going down the country to meet a friend. Her name is Marie, and I haven't seen her in ages. You don't mind, do you?" John kissed her and said he didn't. He said there was a good film on the television over the weekend and that he would watch it.

"That's good," said Ronna, and they continued on walking.

They reached their destination and leaned against the ancient tower, looking out at the rough sea. Seagulls flew above them, and they listened to their loud crying sound.

John was doing his best to hide his sadness and Ronna didn't seem to notice anything different about him.

Later they went for something to eat in the local pub, not Fairley's. John didn't want to go there, and they went to the Seashore bar instead on the main street of the town. There was plenty of room inside and they sat near the fire, surrounded by pictures of Risk from earlier times. Ronna stared at the flames as they waited for the food. They made a glow on her face.

"I love a nice fire," she said, "Peter did too. When we were children, we would sit in front of it for ages and watch the flames dancing. Did you do things like that when you were a child John?"

"Yes," he replied, reflectively, "I still do."

"What do you see when you look?" she asked, becoming all interested in his answer.

"I see lots of things, but I always see your face looking back at me."

She kissed him gently and said, "Thank you, that is so lovely." The food arrived and they tucked in with relish. They were hungry from their walk at Loughsane.

"When do you think you'll hear about if you can stay longer?" asked Ronna. John gave a little laugh.

"What?" she said, looking surprised.

"You say it so easily. You're great. Are you not a bit afraid of all that I've told you, of me being a kind of ghost?"

"You're different, this whole situation is different, but I'm that sort of person. I don't care. When I want something or someone, I just go for it. I have a connection with Peter through you and I'm not giving up on that either."

"I love you," said John, and he started to feel his eyes watering.

"Oh stop, will you, there's no need to get all sad. We'll get through it somehow. They'll let you stay, wait and see."

"Okay then," said john, but in his heart, he knew it wouldn't be like that. He and Ronna would be going their separate ways and there was nothing they could do about it.

They stayed on at the seashore and had a drink. When they came outside it was starting to get dark, and they got into Ronna's car. John held her tightly, so tightly that she felt hardly able to breath.

"Hey, loosen up a bit," she said, releasing herself, "you nearly had the life crushed out of me. It's only for the weekend, I'll be seeing you again on Monday morning. That'll be a new week and we'll see where it takes us." Depression and guilt now started to eat at John, and he felt terrible. He knew though, that he had to hide it from her if he was to get through this. He smiled and fiddled with her hair. Ronna started the car and they soon found themselves at the yard.

"I won't go in," she said, "I've a bag to pack for when I go to Marie's, you don't mind, do you?" John told her he didn't. She told him she would call him on Saturday night. After a few minutes, she drove away and left him standing at the gate. He went inside and stood in the yard. He looked at his watch, it was ten o' clock. He thought about the time he had left. He looked at the office window where Ronna had knocked at to get his attention. It made him incredibly sad. He slowly mounted the steps and stopped under the rusted horseshoe. He touched it and thought about the first day he'd seen it. He opened the red door and went in. He closed it behind him and stood looking into the sitting room. Everything seemed still, silent and lonely. He thought of the journey before him, a journey he would be making very soon and never coming back from.

Chapter 33

The clock said ten minutes to go for his appointment with Rainbow and John closed his eyes. The minutes flew past, and he sensed a presence in front of him. Opening his eyes again, he saw the bearded Rainbow standing in front of him.

"The time has arrived John, you must come with me now." John felt nervous and asked how this was to be done.

"Put your hand on my right shoulder," said Rainbow, "and close your eyes." John did as he was told and felt himself becoming lighter and lighter. He felt afraid, but strangely happy at the same time.

"You can let go now and open your eyes," said Rainbow. It was all over in seconds and John found himself again in the place where he had first met Rainbow. A feeling of joy passed over him, and all his feelings of sadness vanished in an instant.

"I am the gatekeeper," said Rainbow, "I meet souls here and guide them towards that green door over there."

John remembered the door from the last time he was there and how he had chosen not to pass through it.

"This time there is no choice," said Rainbow, "you must now proceed on. This is where we say goodbye." He extended his hand and John shook it, noticing again how cold it felt.

"You needn't worry," said Rainbow, "you will have two reviews, but given how you performed in your new life, I imagine you will pass through quickly. Goodbye, John." And he smiled, pointing the way. John walked to the door, and it opened by itself in front of him. He looked back, but Rainbow was gone. He turned back and walked through the open doorway and stopped. The door closed silently behind him. He saw an armchair facing a wide white cinema- like screen and sat down. There was nothing else in the room except an incredible feeling of peace. Suddenly, and with extraordinary speed, his first life passed in front of him. Everything from his birth to his death appeared on the screen. Despite the speed, John could follow it all clearly without any effort. The swiftness of it didn't seem to matter. It was all very strange.

Soon it was over and at once his life as Mark Foynes started to play on the screen. It all seemed long ago as if it never happened.

When it had finished, a voice in his head told him to enter through another door to his left. He did as he was told and found himself in beautiful countryside. The trees were large and gnarled in a way that made them look like they had faces. A stream flowed gently along between two small hills.

"Over here," came a voice near the stream and John walked in the direction of where it was coming from. A mist formed over the water and a man dressed in a white suit with a wide white hat emerged from it.

"Welcome to the garden of love," he said, in a slow soft voice.

"Are you an angel too?" asked John, feeling elated by everything around him. The man smiled. "Yes, I am Jabez, and you are home now. You have used your second chance well and have no need to stay in the life review process any longer. Go, walk that way." And he pointed to a path that John hadn't noticed before. John took the path that led him by the stream, through the trees, and out into a wide green field. It was filled with Daisies. He sat down on the grass and inhaled the beautiful clear air. He felt happy and everything that had happened to him before seemed to make no difference now. He pulled one of the daisies and looked at it. He had seen thousands of them in life, but now they fascinated him. They were bigger, brighter and seemed to dance before his eyes.

"John?"

He turned in the direction of the voice and Clara was standing behind him. Suddenly, she became the way he'd last seen her all those years ago, and he had changed too without noticing it happening. He jumped up and hugged her.

"Clara," he said emotionally, "oh I'm sorry, so sorry, can you forgive me?"

"There is no need for any forgiveness," she said, smiling, "we will progress here together in this lovely place. Come with me now for always and let us not walk away from each other ever again." He took her hand and they walked across the wide daisy filled field to a small white wooden house with a red brick chimney. By the time they reached the house, they had changed back to grown up versions of themselves. They walked up the steps and stood on a veranda. There was a swing-seat held up by chains with large ornate flowerpots on either side. They contained the most beautiful and unusual flowers that John had ever seen.

Clara turned the sparkling glass doorknob and opened the door. She then looked at John. "There is light in your eyes, a light that will guide you from now on. We will never be lost to each other again, John, and will stay here together always." He kissed her gently and together they walked in and closed the door behind them.

Chapter 34

"On a more serious note," said Marie, suddenly changing the subject that they had been talking about, "I was really sorry to hear about Peter. It must have been an awful shock for you all. I'm sorry I wasn't around for the funeral I would have liked to have been there for you." Ronna looked out the window, feeling sad. She imagined her brother's face, smiling, and then it turned to John's. She had decided she wasn't going to tell Marie about what had been going on, but she wanted to talk about John so badly that she couldn't keep it in.

"Yes, it was a terrible blow to us, but I don't want to talk about it tonight," said Ronna. "I've met somebody since."

"Oh," said Marie, all interested. "Would this be a man by any chance?"

"Yes, it is. He's kind, loving and special."

"Special," said Marie, "in what way exactly?"

"Just special, he seems to know things and I feel when he looks into my eyes, that he's looking into my soul."

"Whew, you're too profound for me," said Marie, surprised by Ronna's answer, "it does sound like love though. Where did you meet him, what does he do?" Ronna smiled.

"His name is Mark, sometimes he calls himself John, I think that's his middle name. He works in Clarke's yard. He hasn't been there very long and that's where I met him. I got a job there not too long ago. He's helping me to get the office files in order. I think it was love at first sight for both of us."

"It sounds like it," said Marie, as she ate her peach dessert.

"He was a great help to me after Peter died. I would have been lost without him."

"In what way?" said Marie. Ronna was tempted to tell her everything, but she managed to restrain herself.

"Oh, I don't know exactly, just being there and being strong for me. He made me feel strong too, in a strange kind of way."

"You make him sound like a man of mystery, but I can see you're happy and I'm happy for you," and Marie placed her hand on Ronna's.

"I'm going to give him a quick call, you don't mind, do you?" said Ronna.

"No, go ahead and call John or Mark or whatever his name is." And they both laughed aloud. Ronna took out her mobile phone and went to her list of contacts. John's number was not among them.

"I don't understand this, his number's gone from my contacts. I know it was here."

"Try J and M, maybe it's in one or the other," said Maire, noticing the look of concern on Ronna's face. The number was nowhere to be found.

"There's no point in ringing the office, Joe keeps the key, anyway he wouldn't want me ringing there. It looks like I'm going to have to leave it until I see him on Monday."

"Why would you ring the office," asked Marie, "does he not have a landline number where he lives?"

"He lives over the stores in the yard," replied Ronna, throwing her phone aside in disappointment. "I can't understand what's happened to the number, I must have deleted it or something. Oh God, this is terrible." She was starting to sound frantic.

"It'll be okay, don't worry," said Marie, trying to reassure her. "You'll see him on Monday, and you can explain to him about the phone. He'll understand. From your description of him, he sounds very understanding." Ronna smiled at Marie.

"Yes, that's it, he's very understanding, there's no need for me to worry, you're right. I'll talk to him on Monday."

"Okay then," said Marie, "let's enjoy the rest of our weekend, everything will be okay, you'll see."

"It will," said Ronna, quietly, "everything's okay." But inwardly, she felt worried.

Chapter 35

The weekend passed quickly as they usually do, and Ronna met Dan at the yard beginning his week's work. He waved to her as she came towards him.

"Have you seen Mark yet?" she asked, feeling anxious.

"No," replied Dan, "he's always up and around at this time. His curtains are still closed, probably didn't set his alarm. He better get up before Joe gets here or there'll be war."

Ronna ran up the steps and banged at his door. "Mark, are you awake, can you hear me?" She said Mark because Dan was standing in the yard, listening. She continued to bang at the door but there was no sound from within. She tried to see through a small gap in the curtains, but she couldn't make anything out. She then tried to force the door open while shouting his name over and over. Dan looked on, baffled by her panic.

Joe arrived in the yard and asked them what the hell they were doing. They explained, and Joe unlocked the office and went in to get a second key to John's home.

He came out again, grumbling about all the bother of it. He climbed the steps and Ronna stood aside. Joe opened the door with the key and they both went in. There was no sign of John, and his bed hadn't been slept in. His wallet was on the table, and it contained nothing. His bag, clothes and passport were gone.

"This is very strange," said Joe. Ronna's mind was racing, and it began to dawn on her, what had happened. "Maybe he's left a message on the phone in the office," she said with desperation in her voice.

"I don't usually encourage it," said Joe, impatiently, "but come down to the office and we'll find out." She followed him down the steps, her legs shaking beneath her.

They passed into the inner office and Joe listened at the phone. There was a short message from John saying he had to go away and would not be back. He thanked Joe for the job. Rainbow had created the message. Ronna went out to her desk and slumped into the swivel chair. She began to cry and Dan, who had followed them in, gave her a glass of water. After a few minutes, she stopped crying and sat with a shocked look on her face. She sipped the water and gazed at the window from where she often saw John working in the yard. She thought of how happy she'd been, but now she felt crushed.

"You just sit there for a while," said Joe, "and I'll go up to the glasshouses and ask the lads if they know anything." He left her and told Dan to hang around the yard just in case Ronna needed him. He got into one of the tractors and drove off.

Ronna didn't know why, but she felt a strong urge to open the drawer in her desk. By this stage, the blood had drained from her face, and she looked the colour of snow. She pulled the drawer open slowly and saw the envelope and large red feather that had been placed there by Rainbow. She knew instantly they were from John. She picked them both up and looked at them. She put the feather down and opened the envelope. She started to read, and her hand shook so badly, that she found it hard to hold the letter steady.

"Hello," came the voice of Caroline from outside the door, "are you there, Joe?" Ronna hadn't heard the van coming into the yard.

When Caroline came in and saw Ronna she gasped. "What's going on? You look terrible."

"I think I know what's happened," said Ronna, her eyes staring blankly. "Come over here, I particularly want you to see this." Caroline sat down beside her and together they both read the letter from John. When they had finished reading it, Caroline tried to comfort Ronna.

"It's a very sad letter to get," said Caroline, "I know how you felt about Mark or John or whatever his name really was. I liked him a lot too, but I still don't believe he was being honest. There is a rational explanation for all this."

"Get out," shouted Ronna.

"I'm sorry you feel that way," said Caroline, and she left the office, banging the door closed behind her. Ronna sat sipping the water slowly, while rubbing the feather across her troubled brow.

Chapter 36

A year passed and Ronna was still working in Clarkes. She drove in and out to work with two feathers in her pocket now. When she was alone, she would hold one in each hand and think of Peter and John. She wondered what they were doing and what their spirit lives were like. Every night, she would go to bed at the same time and ask for them to send her a message. She felt herself more drawn to the feather from John. Ronna didn't feel she could find a love that would replace John's and as a result, became deeply unhappy.

Joe had retired and Ronna had been put in charge of the yard. She liked the job but found it hard with all the reminders of John around the place. A replacement for him had been found, a local man called Des McGivern. He was married and living on the outskirts of the town with a young family. Dan and the others were still working in the yard and found their working life a bit easier now. Ronna didn't bark like Joe, and for that they were grateful. John's room wasn't lived in again after he'd gone. Ronna didn't want anybody else using it. It remained just as he'd left it. When nobody was around, she would go up the stone steps and walk in. Sometimes she imagined she could feel John's presence. She visualised him sitting at the kitchen table drinking tea or watching television. She carried out this ritual everyday despite the fact that it made her feel depressed.

Caroline had left her parent's shop and gone away with Clair Frawley. They planned to stay away for two years, travelling and working abroad. Caroline called it the great adventure. John, or Mark as she knew him, came to her mind from time to time, but on the whole, she tried not to think about him too much. Clair saw her travels as a much-needed break from her acting work. Caroline asked her father to keep an eye on the lighthouse while she and Clair were away.

In the spirit world, John and Clara existed in bliss. They needed nothing more to make their happiness complete. John no longer had any connection to earth, but he did have the power to see what was happening there. At times, he looked in on his family and on Ronna. His family were faring okay, and he watched them putting flowers on his grave. He was happy that they hadn't forgotten him. Ronna was not doing so well, and her sadness bothered him. He knew she was wrestling with her grief and losing the contest. The time was passing, but Ronna was not moving with it.

One evening after a joyful day walking in the garden of love, John and Clara sat in their small wooden house, reading. John put down his book and stared at a painting of a landscape hanging on the wall. Clara looked at him and noticed his unease.

"What is it that troubles you?" she asked.

"I can't stop thinking of Ronna. I see her from time to time when I look down and a dark cloud hangs over her."

"It is hard for her, but hopefully she will find happiness again, you did," replied Clara.

"When I first met Rainbow," said John, "he told me that I would no longer have any connection to earth after I left it the second time. I accepted this, but I feel I need to help Ronna in some way. I want to help take away the darkness that's surrounding her." Clara put down the book she was reading,

"You are a kind loving man, John. I don't know what you can do, but you could talk to Rainbow again. Maybe he can help."

"I lived on earth for a long time in a false belief that I was happy when I knew I wasn't," said John. "I see now how wrong that was, and how it took me down the wrong path and held me back. I don't want Ronna to live that way."

"Yes," replied Clara, picking up her book again, "so many people pretend to be happy with their lives, yet never admit the truth. It's usually the case that they don't want to be pitied or to be seen to be letting the side down. I once spoke to a soul here who told me he'd received lavish gifts and presents in life once he learned to do as he was told. I felt sorry for him and saw how this had been a huge obstruction to his finding true happiness. He needed to learn that nobody had any power over him. Unfortunately, it was only when he came here that he realised it. People feel stuck in their situations but don't want anyone to know. They often carry this off well to those around them but not to themselves." John stood up and moved nearer to the painting. He took a closer look and observed its beautiful trees and bright cornfield. "Earth is lovely, and it can be a very happy place to be, if people are truly honest with themselves."

"That's very profound and also very simple," said Clara, "but you need to have this conversation with Rainbow." John bent down to where she was sitting and kissed her forehead. "When did you become so wise?" he asked. Clara laughed. "Earlier than you. I made mistakes in life too, but when I came here, I could see everything much more clearly. I didn't have somebody in heaven keeping an eye on me. Ronna Smyth is lucky to have met you and to have you here watching over her. Go to Rainbow and let me get on with my book. You'll find him in the halls of glass today, I saw him there earlier." John left Clara and went off in search of Rainbow.

Chapter 37

John made his way to the halls of glass and searched for Rainbow. He found him standing in front of one of the huge stained-glass windows with a white beam of light shining through it. It made the angel shine brightly. He seemed lost in meditation and John approached slowly. Rainbow turned his head in John's direction and stepped away from the light.

"You probably know why I'm here," said John, "being able to read minds."

"No," said Rainbow, "when you came to dwell here, the mind reading stopped. That is only necessary when a soul is still connected to earth. I could read your thoughts the first time I met you because the board had decided you were going back to earth. So, you see you were still connected, we knew you would want to return. At this present moment, I have no idea why you are here. I can only give you a little time, as I have to go and meet some souls who are about to cross over. Please sit down and tell me what's on your mind." They sat on two large bright blue glass chairs facing each other. Rainbow put his fingertips together and waited for John to begin. John told him of Ronna's life now and how unhappy she was. He told Rainbow that he wanted to help her find a path to happiness. Rainbow was silent as John spoke and waited for him to finish. He then leaned forward in the chair, "Have you told me everything that is on your mind? Apart from Ronna's condition in life, are you happy here?"

"Oh yes," replied John, "I have never known such happiness before, and finding Clara again has been so wonderful." Rainbow sat back again. "Good, I'm glad to hear it. You know of course that you are finished with that life on earth, both as John Hughes and Mark Foynes. I did tell you that you would have no more connection with life on earth when you got here." John grew uneasy and anticipated a refusal at being allowed to help Ronna. Rainbow took a large blue coloured handkerchief from his pocket and began to shine the silver buttons on his coat. When he'd finished, he put the handkerchief in his pocket again and looked at John. "I tell you again, you cannot go back to earth. You have already had a chance at life a second time and it worked well for you. However, your concern for Ronna is touching and it's hard to disregard it. Perhaps there is another way."

John grew excited. "What is it?" he asked, anxiously.

"Ronna, like everybody else on earth has a spirit guide. Whether she listens to him or not is a matter for herself. His name is Roger. He lived a long and happy life when on earth and has been here a long time. Perhaps if you were to talk with him about Ronna you might come to some sort of arrangement. It's worth a try, don't you think?"

"Yes, oh yes," replied John, hardly managing to contain his excitement. "Where will I find him?"

"He is sure to be in the rambling fields. He goes there a lot to contemplate when he takes a break from guiding. Yes, I'm certain you will find him there close to the wheel of grace. You can't miss it. It's a big wooden structure painted red and yellow and turning in the stream of glory. I must hurry away now as I'm expecting one of those souls who didn't feel he was good enough in his earth existence. Insidious behaviour brought on by an inferiority complex would be the exact description. It made him resentful, mean, spiteful and jealous, bad traits. He hid his feelings of inadequacy well, but in private, he suffered needlessly. He'll feel so regretful when it's all clearly revealed to him in the review process and wonder how he could have been so blind. Good luck with Roger." And Rainbow vanished.

John went back to his quaint home and found Clara sitting on the swing seat on the porch. He told her about his conversation with Rainbow.

"So, there's hope then," said Clara. "Come and sit beside me and talk with Roger tomorrow." John sat down, and together they watched the silver rings dancing in the sky.

Chapter 38

The following day, John made his way to the rambling hills. They were beautiful and covered in soft green grass surrounded by blackberry bushes. After walking a short distance, he came upon the huge mill wheel that Rainbow had described, turning in the stream of glory. Sitting beside the creaking structure was a man dressed in a black cloak with stars on it. He was writing something in a brown covered book that was perched on his knee. He looked up when he saw John approaching.

"Hello," said John, suddenly feeling shy, "are you Roger?"

"Yes, that's right, I'm Roger, and who are you?" Before John could answer, the spirit guide jumped to his feet and shook John's hand. He seemed the quick moving nervous type, but friendly in an odd sort of way. There was a large rock nearby and he told John to sit on it.

"So, who are you, and why do you want to talk to me?" asked Roger.

"I'm John Hughes, I haven't been here a very long time and I wanted to ask a favour from you. It concerns Ronna Smyth; I was close to her. She's not happy and I want to help her."

"Of course," said Roger, "now I recognise you. I'm sorry I didn't know you for a moment there, you look happier. There is light in your eyes. I know your story because I am the spirit guide for Ronna, which you already know of course or else you wouldn't be here talking to me."

"Yes, that's right," said John, not knowing what to make of Roger. The spirit guide scratched his shaggy head with the pen and looked John up and down. "As I said, I am Ronna's guide and as such, it's my job to help her on her journey through life. Are you looking for my job?"

"Oh no, of course not," replied John. "It's just that I feel very concerned for her and can see the unhappy state she's in. I was given a second chance at life and found happiness. I would like to do something for her now and help her find happiness too just as I did."

"Ah, I see," said Roger, drawing his cloak closer around him. "The trouble is if you are to take on this task, then what would I do?" John was silent; he didn't know how to answer this. Roger smiled at him. "Don't speak for a minute, wait and think about what you want to say. I'll continue with my writing here." He opened his book again and started to write.

Five minutes passed, and John stood up. "I have an idea," he said. Roger closed his book again and put down his pen.

"What is it?" he asked.

"Do you think we could work together? I know Ronna so well, and perhaps I could help guide you so that you can get her to take heed of your guidance. Isn't it true that people often ignore the messages that guides send them? You know her as your subject, I know her personally. I feel this could be a win for both of us." Roger stood up and walked towards the revolving wheel. He stood for a few minutes watching it turn and scoop up the water. He turned slowly and faced John with a slight smile of his face. "Yes, I think we might do something together. I'm beginning to like your plan, John. I'll have to take it up with the board, so I can't guarantee anything. We do know though that they are open to other ways from the chance you were given at a second life. By the way, I imagine that must have been a fascinating experience." John told him it was, and how he had found out the importance of not rejecting true love.

"Yes, yes of course," said Roger, "let me talk to the board and we'll take it from there. They might agree, but they might say it's my job to guide Ronna. Be prepared for anything."

"Thank you so much," said John, "I look forward to working with you."

"We'll see, we'll see," said Roger, "now if you don't mind, I must continue with my writing." He opened his book again and didn't speak anymore. John left him and walked back across the lush hills towards his little house.

Chapter 39

It was five days later when John heard again from Roger. Clara had gone out for a walk, and John sat in an armchair gazing into the fire that was now burning brightly. A knock came to the door, and on answering it, he found Roger standing on the porch. John invited him in, and the two men sat down.

"That's a nice fire you have there," said Roger. "Heaven can be a cold place at times, weather wise that is. Who would believe it?"

"Yes indeed," replied John, "I take it you have some news from the board for me." Roger sniffed in a self-important way and cleared his throat.

"I have, and would you believe it, they have agreed. It's taken them this long, but they have kindly decided to let us work together for the benefit of Ronna Smyth." John was delighted and asked when they could begin their work.

"Now, if you like," replied Roger, "I have my pen and book with me. I know things about Ronna of course. I took her on about three years ago. I know about her brother Peter dying, that was a sad business. She was devastated. He's here amongst us, have you met him?"

"No," replied John, "it might be a good idea if I did, he could be helpful."

"We'll see," said Roger. "What really stands out in your mind when you think of Ronna?" John answered immediately. "Her kindness, innocence and ability to truly love. Something else besides all that, the importance she attaches to feathers."

"Oh yes," said Roger, "there was that business with the feathers. That was a nice touch."

"She carries one from me everywhere she goes and the one she thinks came from her brother. She worships them, and they have kept her going in this gloomy time. I think more feathers would work wonders for her." Roger tapped the pen against his teeth in thought. "Yes, I think that's good. I will see she is surrounded with feathers. Being the type of person she is, she'll have no doubt where they came from. Does it have to be a particular type of feather?"

"I would think white ones with black tips and red ones the best, they'll mean something to her," replied John. Roger wrote it down in his book and closed it. "Please stay quiet, John, just for a moment while I concentrate." Roger closed his eyes, and a white-coloured aura surrounded him. It lasted for seconds, and then suddenly disappeared. There was a knock at the door.

"That will be Peter, Ronna's brother, I summoned him here just now."

"Oh," said John, "that's a surprise." He went to the door and opened it. A man aged about thirty stood outside. He resembled Ronna, and his eyes radiated kindness. He smiled at John.

"I've been told to come here by somebody called Roger, are you him?"

"No, he's inside, I'm John, pleased to meet you." And they shook hands. "Please come in." Peter walked into the room followed by John.

"Ah, Peter Smyth," said Roger, rising from his chair, "thank you for coming, we've just been discussing your sister Ronna." Peter's face grew serious.

"Please tell me she's not here. I would love to see her again, but I'm hoping she hasn't died already."

"No, no nothing like that," replied Roger, "sit down please." They all three sat down and looked at each other. Roger explained who he and John were and why they were taking such an interest in Ronna. Peter listened with fascination. John explained how a feather had been sent to Ronna and how she believed it came from Peter.

"I wanted to send her a sign," said Peter, looking down at the floor in an embarrassed way, "but because I committed a serious offence in life, I don't yet have the ability to see or send messages to her. I have to walk the avenue of atonement for another while yet."

"What was the offence?" asked John. Peter looked uncomfortable and ashamed.

"I took a lot of money which wasn't mine. I was told when I got here that my soul would need to be fully cleansed before I was ready to move on to the next stage. You see, I didn't right the wrong on earth. I intended to, but then I got sick and died quickly. The chance was lost. Because of this I must wait and have no knowledge as to how my family are coping with my shame."

"I can see you're not a bad sort," said Roger, "a moment of madness, I would say. You'll get there, have no fear. There is love and forgiveness here, but you must understand wrong doing has to be addressed."

"I do understand," said Peter, "and every day, I walk the avenue reflecting on my action. I am constantly contrite and asking for forgiveness."

"Anyway," said Roger in an official tone, "we're not here today to talk about you. Is there anything you can tell us about Ronna? Did you for instance have any special connection between you? What makes her happy, etcetera?"

"It would be an immense help to all of us and Ronna if you could tell us anything," said John. Peter looked out the window and seemed lost in thought. He imagined Ronna when they were younger and tried to remember what she liked. "I'm seeing her walking on the beach and fire. She always liked a nice fire and she used to say it made her feel cosy and happy. When we were children, we often imagined we could see pictures in the fire at home."

"Yes, that's true," said John, "she told me about that."

"You mentioned the beech, did she walk there much?" said Roger.

"Yes," replied Peter, "we didn't live too far from it and any chance she got, she would be out walking on the sand in her bare feet."

"Thank you, Peter," said Roger, "your information has been very valuable. We may speak with you again soon. In the meantime, I as Ronna's spirit guide and John here as a former loved one will do our best to steer her towards happiness again."

"I would like very much for that to happen," said Peter, standing up to leave. John showed him to the door, and they shook hands.

"Don't worry," said John, "Ronna is in good hands."

"Thank you," said Peter and he walked away from the house feeling hopeful. As John turned to go back in, Roger was standing behind him. He put his hand on John's shoulder and said, "We'll begin our work as soon as possible, but now I must be away to the hills again. We'll speak presently." And he left John feeling optimistic.

Chapter 40

Caroline woke with a loud shout and jumped out of bed. She ran from the bedroom and burst into Clair's bedroom in a panic like state. They were now working together in an insurance office in Paris and renting a flat in Montmartre. They had travelled to Croatia, Spain and France since leaving home, and were now enjoying living in the famous district of the city.

"What is it, what's wrong, did you have a nightmare?" said Clair, turning on the bedside lamp. Caroline threw herself on Clair's bed and they embraced each other.

"I had a terrible dream," said Caroline, releasing Clair again, "that I was locked in a huge glasshouse and the heat was unbearable. There were hundreds of tomatoes piled all around me and under my feet. The tomatoes on the ground started to move and Mark emerged from them. He came towards me and put his hands on my shoulders. My story is true," he said in an angry way. "He shook me with force as if to make me believe him and then I woke."

"Thankfully, it was only a dream," said Clair, in a rational voice, "from what I saw of him, he meant you no harm. For some reason, he just couldn't be truthful with you. I thought you'd forgotten all about him."

"I had forgotten him, but now and again he comes to mind. The other day I thought I saw him in the street. It wasn't him of course, but just for a moment I thought it was. Sometimes I think Mark was some sort of conman. I don't really know what his angle was though."

"So what," said Clair, "he's gone now, and you just had a bad dream, go back to bed and get some sleep." Caroline rose from the bed and walked towards the door but turned back again and sat on Clair's bed.

"What if it's true that he was let live again to find love. The dream felt so real. I felt it meant something."

"Well," said Clair, impatiently and wanting to go back to sleep, "I can't tell you anymore about him. From what I could see, Mark Foynes didn't exist. The strange thing is if he wasn't Mark Foynes, I would still pick up things from the lines on his palm. There was nothing. It doesn't make sense. Why not forget him once and for all? We came here to have new adventures can't you just banish him from your mind?"

"No, I can't," replied Caroline irritably. "Two streets away from where we are now, there is a woman known as Madame Valadon. She can contact the dead and can speak English. I'm going to make an appointment to see her, will you come with me?"

"Okay, I will, but I think you're being ridiculous, Mark is not dead, so how is she going to contact him?" Caroline didn't reply.

"I'll go with you," said Clair, "and watch you waste your money, but can we go back to sleep now?" She lay down again, made a sighing sound and shut her eyes.

"Goodnight," said Caroline, "and thanks for being a friend. I'll contact her tomorrow." She shut the bedroom door and returned to her room. She got into bed and turned the bedside lamp off. She thought about the dream, and it made her shudder. A strong curiosity gripped her as to the true identity of Mark Foynes and if his story was true.

"It can't be," she said over and over, until she fell asleep.

Chapter 41

The following day was Friday and Caroline made her way to the home of Madame Valadon on her way home from work. She had heard so many stories about the renowned psychic from the people in the office where she worked and how they were all convinced of Madame Valadon's powers. She found the house in a narrow-cobbled street and rang the doorbell. An old woman with a coloured shawl around her shoulders answered the door. She stood looking at Caroline with a curious look on her face.

"Hello, are you Madame Valadon?" said Caroline, feeling nervous.

"That is correct," answered Madame Valadon. "I am she, what do you want with me?" Caroline felt a bit taken of guard; she was not expecting to see the famous medium opening the door. It seemed too ordinary a task for a woman with her reputation. "I was wondering if I could make an appointment to see you, perhaps tomorrow if that would suit."

"Tomorrow does not suit me," replied Madame Valadon, "I can see you now if you wish."

"Yes, yes indeed," said Caroline, "I thought I would have to wait longer before seeing you. My friend agreed to come along with me, but we thought it would be a few more days before I got an appointment."

"We don't need anybody else with us when I do a sitting. Please come in." Caroline walked in and Madame Valadon closed the heavy old door behind her.

"This way please." And Caroline followed her up narrow stairs to a room with a white panelled door. Madame Valadon opened the door, and they went inside. The room was bright and cheerful and prints of paintings by Renoir and Lautrec hung on the wall. There was a polished round table in the middle of the room and a lighted candle was placed on it in a brass holder.

"Please sit down at the table," said Madame Valadon. Caroline did as she was told, and the medium sat opposite her. "Tell me what it is that you want," said Madame Valadon in a matter-of-fact way. Caroline opened her handbag and pulled out the red handkerchief that had been placed in her drawer at home in Risk. "Can you tell me where this has come from and who it belongs to." Madame Valadon took the handkerchief from Caroline and examined it closely.

"I would have thought you knew that if it was in your bag. Okay, don't say anything more." She stood up and closed the curtains. She sat down again closed her eyes and began to breath, deeply.

Five minutes passed and Caroline sat nervously on the edge of the chair, staring at Madame Valadon and at the artist prints on the wall. The distinguished medium stood up and opened the curtains again. She sat back down and handed the handkerchief back to Caroline. "This handkerchief," she began, "came from the spirit world. It never existed here on earth or belonged to anybody. It was sent to you as a sign that life exists beyond death. Am I correct?" Caroline was in shock and didn't answer immediately. "I asked you am I correct?" said Madame Valadon in a firm voice.

"Yes, you are, but I can hardly believe it."

"You don't have to if you don't want to," said Madame Valadon in a non-caring voice, "my fee is still one hundred euro." Caroline opened her purse and gave the money to Madame Valadon. The old lady took it and placed it in a small yellow tin box that was on a stool close to where she was sitting. "Where did you get this handkerchief?" Caroline told her everything that had happened since she met Mark.

"It is indeed a very strange tale," said Madame Valadon. "Before you leave here, I want you to know that what I have told you is true. Now that you have this knowledge, what do you intend to do with it?" Caroline held the handkerchief tightly in her hand.

"I don't know, it's such a strange feeling. Thank you for your time." She stood up to go and Madame Valadon went ahead down the stairs and opened the front door. The noise of the street made everything seem so normal again to Caroline.

"Goodbye and thank you," said Caroline, "you have given me much to think about."

"Goodbye," said Madame Valadon, "call to me again if you feel you need to," and she shut the door.

Chapter 42

When Caroline arrived home, her mind was in a whirl. She believed what Madame Valadon had told her, but at the same time she couldn't fully accept it. She sat down to dinner with Clair and didn't speak for five minutes. Clair guessed something had happened and wondered was it a problem at work. "How was your day?" asked Clair, leaving down her knife and fork.

"Work was fine," answered Caroline, "but on the way home, I called to Madame Valadon to make an appointment. She took me by surprise and told me to come in."

"Oh really," said Clair, "did you have a sitting with her or whatever mediums call it?"

"I showed her the red handkerchief that Mark claimed had come from my spirit guide. I don't know why I ever kept it. She told me it came from the spirit world and was a sign to me that there is life after death."

"As a palm reader," said Clair, "I believe in the afterlife, but I've never been able to accept Mark's story. I mean really, who would?"

"I felt that way too, and yet Madame Valadon has said the handkerchief has come from the spirit world. Mark or whatever his name is, told me that I would get a sign if I asked, and I did. Now I'm thinking that maybe there is something in it after all." Clair resumed eating and looked at Caroline who was lost in thought.

"Why are you looking at me like that?" asked Caroline.

"Because I know what you're thinking. You want to go back to Ireland again, am I right?"

"I don't know why exactly or what difference it'll make, but yes, I do. I feel unsettled by all this."

"It just so happens," said Clair, "that my agent sent me a text this morning. There's a film that's being shot in Dublin in the next few months. I've been asked am I interested."

"Are you interested?" asked Caroline.

"I'm very interested. I'd like to stay here longer, but this film is something I can't turn down. Well, it looks like we're going. I know exactly what I'm going back to, but I'm concerned about you. You'll find life in the shop a bit dull after Paris."

"I know," said Caroline, "but I want to talk to Ronna Smyth again, I feel I have to. This whole business is bugging me."

"Don't say anything more," said Clair, "we'll make the arrangements, and I'll tell my agent to expect me soon."

"Thank you," said Caroline, and she stood up from the table. She went over to where she'd left her handbag. She opened it and took the red handkerchief out. She held it to her forehead and looked from the window down at the busy Parisian Street in a reflective way.

Chapter 43

Ronna was busy in the office when she heard a van coming into the yard. She came out and met Jack Finnegan opening the doors to his van and loading up boxes of tomatoes. Dan was helping him.

"It's all there, Jack," she said, pointing to the boxes. "I'll leave you in the safe hands of Dan."

"That's fine, Ronna, I'll be gone in a few minutes. Oh by the way, my daughter is coming home next week, so you'll probably see her coming into the yard from now on." Ronna thought of the last time she'd seen Caroline and how she'd told her to get out of the office. She remembered showing Caroline the letter from John and how annoyed she'd been by Caroline's reaction to it. Ronna didn't say anything more to Jack and went back into the office. She sat down and began inputting invoices on to the computer.

After twenty minutes had passed, she heard the van driving away and the yard was quiet. The mention of Caroline's name had brought John to mind, and she came back out to the yard again. Dan wasn't there, and the other workers were all working in the fields and glasshouses. She looked towards what used to be John's room and felt something telling her that she should go in. She went up the stone steps and opened the door slightly. Ronna sensed a strange feeling coming over her, and she held the doorknob tightly in her hand. She pushed the door further back and was astonished to see a pile of feathers on the bed. She rushed across the room and picked them up. Some were red, and the others were white with black tips. She sat down on the bed and smiled. "You're somewhere out there, aren't you John, and so is Peter. What am I to do, please tell me?" she said to herself. "Where do I go from here? Please come to me, now right away." She waited and listened, but nothing happened. She stood up and stuffed the feathers in her pockets. She then stood in front of the mirror and thought of how John had stood there, shaving. Ronna didn't know it, but Roger was standing behind her. She couldn't see him as she had not yet passed through death, but she did feel that she was being shown signs for a reason. As she stood looking at her reflection, she began to imagine the years ahead going on and on without John. Ronna felt her life had become a tragedy and she feared for the future. She felt at a loss and that she had been robbed of love, a love she felt that was true and good. "We had something special, John and I," she said to herself, "and now it's taken away." She then thought of Caroline, and it made her angry. "I'll never talk to her again, I hate her," she said out loud. Ronna heard somebody coming up the steps and she turned towards the door, it was Dan.

"Oh, it's you, Ronna. I thought I heard somebody talking. This old room hasn't changed at all. I'm sure you still miss Mark."

"Yes, I do," replied Ronna, "don't you have any work to do?" Dan didn't say anything more and hurried down the steps again. Ronna lay on the bed, which was quite dusty now and imagined herself in the arms of John. She hugged the yellowing pillow and began to cry. She stayed there until all the workers had gone home. It was dark before she came down again. She stood looking around the yard and at the red door at the top of the steps. She then got into her car and set off for home.

Chapter 44

Three weeks later, Caroline and Clair arrived home. It was very late at night when they landed in Dublin airport, and Caroline had decided she would stay with Clair in the lighthouse until the morning. She didn't want to wake her parents in the middle of the night. She had sent her mother a text from Paris, letting her know of this arrangement.

A taxi dropped them at the lighthouse, and they paid the driver. "Do you live here?" he asked.

"I do," said Clair. He seemed amazed. "Wow, I never met anybody who lived in a lighthouse, bye now." And he drove off, leaving them in darkness. Clair rummaged in her bag for the key to the door.

"Don't go in yet," said Caroline, "let's just stand here for a minute." They both stood in silence and looked out at the blackness where the sea was. They could just about make out the shape of the island and the Martello tower which was a short distance away.

"Come on," said Clair, "I'm getting cold." She turned the key in the door, and they went inside. Clair told

Caroline to follow her up to the second landing to where the bedrooms were. She opened a door and showed Caroline where she would be sleeping. "You get yourself ready for bed, and I'll just throw my stuff into my room. I'll meet you downstairs in a few minutes and we'll have a cup of tea." Caroline took her pyjamas from her case and quickly changed into them. She looked around the room and thought how it might be nice to live in a lighthouse. There was a wardrobe with flowers painted on it. Caroline thought it looked very unusual. She opened it and saw a pile of theatre programmes from different plays that Clair had acted in over the years. She closed it again and heard Clair calling to her that the tea was ready.

Caroline went back down the winding stairs and found her friend, putting a teapot and biscuits on the table. She was dressed in a long dark dressing gown with large white designs sown on to it.

"Ah, there you are," said Clair, "sit down and let's drink this tea, I'm dying for a cup. I always find I get very dry on a flight; tea revives me."

"This is a lovely place to live," said Caroline, sitting down and pouring the tea. "Do you ever get lonely here?"

"Sometimes," replied Clair, munching on a biscuit, "but Tom comes over sometimes and then I'm not lonely."

"Who's Tom?" asked Caroline. "I never heard you mention him before." Clair got up from the table and opened a drawer in the cabinet. She came back to the table and handed Caroline a photograph of a man. He had long hair and a moustache, Caroline thought he looked arty. "Is he a boyfriend?" she asked.

"Kind of," replied Clair, "nothing too serious yet. He acts too, and I met him on a film set. He's kind and caring, and I like him a lot. I've got something else to show you."

"Oh." Clair took a small notebook from her dressing gown pocket. "These are some notes I made after your visit with Mark, the day you called here. I didn't mention them before because I didn't want to upset you. I hope I'm not doing the wrong thing in showing them to you now." Caroline looked pleasantly surprised.

"No, not at all, tell me what you've written." Clair opened the notebook and began to read.

"I had a visit from Caroline a few days ago. She brought a friend with her called Mark Foynes. I tried to read his palm. I could find nothing in it. There was no past, present or future visible in the lines on his hand. When I pointed this out, he seemed anxious to leave. Caroline thinks he has something to hide and has broken off her friendship with him. It is clear to me that he is not who he says he is, but who is he? Even if he's not Mark Foynes, he must be somebody. Is he a ghost? He looks to solid to be one. I don't think he means harm, but I am concerned for Caroline. He seems to have unsettled her. I have consulted with another friend about this who is very good at unusual cases. She thinks that there may be something in the story that he gave Caroline, that is, he died and was let live again in order to feel love. I'm not sure how I can help Caroline." Clair closed the notebook and put it down on the table in front of her.

"Do you agree with your friend?" asked Caroline.

"Let me put it in this way," replied Clair. "He came here, I read his palm and there was nothing. It's not possible. It's as though he was placed here on earth. He's told you a tale, which you find impossible to believe. There are two impossibilities, but I'm beginning to think one of them is true. He struck me as a truthful person when I met him, yet what he says sounds like nonsense. He's gone, and I'm wondering should we just drop this now and not talk about it anymore."

"I can't," said Caroline, "and for two reasons. He's in my head now and he's not going away. The second is because I knew and liked him before Ronna Smyth ever saw him. I feel she knows more about this than me, and I don't like that."

"That may be true," said Clair, "but remember he found love with her and then he vanished again. Perhaps his mission was over."

"He found love with me first," said Caroline, with irritation in her voice. "I want to speak to Ronna Smyth again." Clair stood up and walked to where her friend was sitting and put her arms around her.

"Why don't we leave it for now. Get a good night's sleep, maybe it'll be clearer in your head when you get up in the morning." Caroline smiled and they left the table to go to their rooms.

Chapter 45

One day, Ronna was sitting in the office. She was thinking about John and remembering nice times they'd spent together. She tapped the pen she was holding on the screen of her mobile phone, when suddenly an idea came to her. "Of course," she said to herself, "why didn't I think of it sooner." She had suddenly remembered John telling her the date of his death. She had a good head for dates, and she quickly went into the RIP website on her phone. She entered John's name and details, and immediately his death notice appeared on the screen. She saw that he had lived in the city in a flat and the name of the undertakers who had organised his funeral. She also saw that he had died in a hospital and that he had a family. She rang the undertakers and was answered by a man with a kind sounding voice. Ronna explained that she was a close friend of John's. She said she'd been abroad for a couple of years and had only just returned and heard about John dying. She said she wanted to send her condolences to the family but had mislaid their address and was wondering would the undertakers give it to her.

"I'm afraid I can't give out that information," answered the man with the kind voice, "but I can give you a phone number for John's parents."

"That would be very helpful," said Ronna. The undertaker called out the number, and Ronna wrote it down on a scrap of paper, "oh, by the way, can you tell me where John was buried?" The undertaker asked her to hold on for a minute. She could hear him opening a drawer and rummaging through papers. He came back to the phone. "He was buried in Mount Jerome cemetery." Ronna thanked him and she ended the phone call. All kinds of thoughts passed through her mind, but she felt an urge to ring the number that the undertaker had given her.

There was knock at the office door, and Ronna said come in. The door opened and Caroline Finnegan came into the dingy office.

"What do you want," said Ronna, in a hostile voice.

"I won't take long," answered Caroline, "I just want to talk about Mark Foynes or whoever he really is."

"He's gone, and what do you care anyway?"

"Do you know where he's gone?"

"Yes, I do as a matter of fact. He's gone back to the spirit world, and you know it too, so why are you asking?"

"You know I don't believe that stupid story that he told us, and I wonder if you really do either," said Caroline.

"I do believe it," said Ronna, "what's it to you anyway? You didn't show him much understanding when he was here, and you lost him to me."

"We might have worked something out in time if you hadn't stolen him from me."

"Well, he's gone now and he's not coming back," said Ronna.

"I think you're lying and that you know where he really is. I want to know."

"I already told you, so there's nothing more to say, is there?"

Caroline left the office and slammed the door behind her. Ronna watched her from the window and saw her walking hurriedly across the yard. She went back to the desk and picked up the scrap of paper with the phone number that she'd been given by the undertakers. She dialled the number and a woman's voice answered. "Hello."

"Hello," answered Ronna, "I'm an old friend of John's and I just heard of his passing. Please accept my condolences. I got your number from the undertakers. I hope you don't mind me calling."

"Not at all. I'm John's mother. We were all very sad when he died and were with him in the hospital at the time. You're very kind to call."

"I was wondering if I could call around and tell you in person how sorry I am. Would that be okay?"

"Of course, there's no need really to put yourself to that trouble, but if you want to. Do you have a pen?"

"Yes," said Ronna. John's mother called out the address and Ronna wrote it down.

"Would it be all right to come tomorrow around three o'clock?" said Ronna.

"That's fine, we'll see you then, bye now." And Ronna heard the line going dead. She now had the date John died, where he was buried and his parents phone number and address. "All I have left to do is call," she said to herself and smiled at the thought of it.

Chapter 46

The next day, Ronna told the workers that she had business in the city and would be back later. She drove out of the yard wondering how her meeting with John's parents would be. She tried to imagine them and what they would look like. For some reason, she visualised them as strong, honest and kind people. She wondered if she was right. She also wondered why John's life had gone wrong and if his parents had anything to do with it. "Maybe they stood in his way, maybe in some way without knowing it they blocked his path to love," she said to herself as she drove along.

An hour later, she was driving into a large housing estate. She found the house and parked outside. Ronna felt nervous, but then told herself that John would be happy about her visiting his parents. She walked to the bright green front door of the house and knocked. She waited for a moment or two, but there was no answer. She was about to ring again when she heard a stir inside. The door opened and a tall man in a white shirt and black trousers stood facing her.

"Hello," he said, "you must be John's friend, my wife said you'd be calling, come in." Ronna went in and he shut the door behind her. The house had a pleasant, homely feel to it and Ronna imagined she could feel John's presence. She was led into the living room and John's mother was standing on a mat in front of the fireplace. She was of average height, slim and wore large glasses like her husband.

"Hello, Mrs Hughes, I'm Ronna Smyth. Thank you for taking my call the other day."

"Call me Mary, and this is Joe. Sit down, while I get some tea."

"Please don't go to any trouble," said Ronna.

"No trouble at all, it's all ready." She left the room and John's father smiled at Ronna. "It's great to hear John had friends, he didn't get along with people usually." Mary came back into the room carrying a tray with tea and scones on it. "I hope you like scones."

"Oh yes," replied Ronna, "that's lovely, thank you very much." Mary poured the tea and they all sat down.

"So Ronna, tell us how you know John," said Joe. Ronna said she had gone on a few dates with him some years ago and that they had gone their separate ways. She told them she'd gone abroad to work for a year and from time-to-time, John crossed her mind. She said she had only just heard from a friend of hers that John had died and that was why she made contact.

"Well, I must say," said Mary, "this is a pleasant surprise. We never knew John to go out with any girls except maybe his childhood sweetheart."

"Who was she?" asked Ronna.

"Clara Buckley," replied Mary. "Oh she was a lovely girl. They would have been only about thirteen at the time, but they were very close. They were always together, and then suddenly there was a change in John. I don't know what soured him, and then Clara was out of his life. I always felt it was a mistake."

"We both did," said Joe, sounding sad.

"Where is Clara now?" asked Ronna.

"She's been dead a long number of years," replied Mary, "she married when she was very young, but her husband wasn't a very reasonable man. I know it's an awful thing to say, but nobody liked him. She was later diagnosed with cancer and died soon afterwards. She's buried in Mount Jerome cemetery where John is also buried. She was Clara Johnson when she died. She was quite young at the time of her death."

"Did you go out with John for long?" asked Joe, pouring more tea into Ronna's cup.

"We went out a few times, but they were special times. I was very sad to hear that he'd died." Ronna started to feel emotional and stared into space.

"Don't upset yourself," said Mary, "you'll meet somebody else. Can I ask why you parted?"

"It was a disagreement about John going away. I didn't want him to go, but he said he had to and that he probably wouldn't be seeing me for a long time." Joe shifted in his chair, "that's strange, he never mentioned anything about going away to us. On second thoughts, maybe it's not so strange, he became distant from us and the rest of the family and told us nothing."

"Can you tell me where his grave is, I'd like to visit it?" said Ronna.

"If you call at the public office in Mount Jerome graveyard, they'll tell you exactly how to find it," said Mary. Ronna said she had to get back to work and thanked them for allowing her to visit. As she stood up to leave, Mary handed her a small envelope.

"That's a memorial card with John's picture on it, keep it. I reckon after meeting you now, that John was a bit older than you. Well, what of it once you have good memories of him." She gave Ronna a hug and Joe shook her hand.

Ronna went back out to her car and got in. She rolled the window down. "Bye now and thank you so much for the tea and the memorial card." They waved her off and went back into the house. Ronna drove around the corner and stopped. She opened the envelope that John's mother had given her and looked at the picture on the card. She saw a man aged about forty and he didn't look anything like the John she knew. Despite this, she still felt connected to him. "It's what's inside him that counts," she said to herself, "not what he looks like." She kissed the picture and put it back into the envelope.

Twenty minutes later, Ronna was parking her car close to the entrance of Mount Jerome cemetery. She walked a short distance and found the public office. She went in, and a man behind the counter asked if he could help her. She showed him John's memorial card with the date of when he died and asked if she could be directed to his grave. The man looked up the plots on a computer screen and quickly found John's. He scribbled the location of the grave on a piece of paper and handed it to her.

"Thank you," said Ronna, "I'm looking for another grave as well. I don't have details, just a name, Clara Johnson."

"I should be able to find it with the name only." He went to the computer again and after a minute, he found the record. He wrote it down on another piece of paper and handed it to Ronna.

"Thank you," she said and left the office. She followed the directions and five minutes later, she found John's grave. It was marked by a square headstone with a statue of an angel sitting on top. She saw by it that John was forty-five when he died. She touched the stone and looked at the dying flowers on the grave.

"Death was not final for you, was it John?" she said aloud as there was nobody around. "What do I do with myself now? I miss you and want you to come back again. Please, please come back you did before, it's possible." She grew tearful and left the grave in search of Clara's resting place.

She found it on the other side of the graveyard. It looked neglected, and Ronna saw that Clara was only twenty-nine when she died. At the top of the headstone, there was a picture of Clara. She had a wide smile and light-coloured, hair. "So young to die," said Ronna, again out loud. "You both died so young. Are you together now, I wonder?"

Ronna walked back to her car and got in. She didn't know how seeing the graves would really help her, but felt she just had to know where they were buried.

"What next?" she asked herself and drove away from the place of silence.

Chapter 47

A few days later, Caroline was asleep in bed. She had been out late the night before with her friends. She had decided not to set the alarm on the clock and to sleep on until she woke. At one o'clock in the afternoon, she woke to the strong scent of roses in the room. It was overpowering, and she got out of bed and opened the window. As she did so, she noticed the drawer in her dressing table was wide open. She was positive she had closed it the night before and wondered had she walked in her sleep. She went to close it and saw a red envelope inside that hadn't been there the night before. She took it from the drawer and sat on the bed to see what was inside. She opened the envelope and removed a white sheet of paper. It read as follows.

"This note is from me. I am your spirit guide. You don't need to know my name yet. I have been asked by another guide to intervene so that they may help another soul. I have written these words so that you will learn to believe in people. You never were a very trusting person, and it's time for you to change. Not every single thing can be explained rationally. Mark Foynes, as you know him was telling the truth. He lived, he died, and he lived again. He was given a chance to find love, to find what he missed the first time around. Your practical mind and lack of faith has prevented you from believing this. You go to the church on Sundays, and you pray to God and Saints. Saints are people who lived and died, yet we're told they walk amongst us. Lots of people believe this, yet they say they don't believe in spirits. It's just another form of what's called the supernatural. I, as your spirit guide am trying to direct you in your life, but it's up to you really. You must leave Ronna Smyth in peace; she will find her own way as you will yours. If you don't believe, I put this note in the drawer, ask your parents was it them. I'm sure they'll say no, and they are the only other people in the house. Know that I am always with you and learn from this. May you find peace." The note was not signed, and Caroline's hands shook as she tried to put it back into the envelope. She quickly got dressed and rushed downstairs.

"Ah, you're up at last," said her mother.

"I have to rush out," said Caroline, "I'll be back later." Her mother was shouting after her to have some breakfast, but the van drove away quickly from the front of the house.

A short time later, Caroline was running up the hill to the lighthouse. She was excited and wondered what Clair would make of the note. She knocked at the door.

Clair opened the door and saw the look on her friend's face.

"What's happened?" said Clair. "You look different or something, come in." Caroline hurried in and threw herself on the sofa.

"You just have to read this." And she handed Clair the envelope. Caroline couldn't stay sitting from the excitement she was feeling, and she walked around the room in a restless state. Clair read the note slowly, and when she'd finished, she placed it against her forehead.

"What are you doing?" asked Caroline. Clair took the note away again and looked at it. "This note is authentic. We've learned something here, especially you."

"I know," said Caroline, "and somehow, I believe it. It's goes against all logic and reason, but I feel it is true."

"Will you learn from it?" asked Clair. "And will you leave Ronna Smyth alone?"

"Yes, I will, and it'll make me look at things differently from now on."

"I'm glad you said that. This has been a lesson for both of us. Perhaps Mark Foynes has found his true path at last."

"Here's to future happiness for us all," said Caroline, "no more looking back. Let's shake on it." They shook hands and smiled at each other.

Chapter 48

John and Clara were sitting on the swing seat outside their heavenly home. Roger suddenly appeared and sat beside them on a small barrel.

"Ah, John and Clara," said Roger, "you both look very contented sitting there with each other. I have news on Caroline Finnegan."

"Oh," said John, "what can that be?" He was wishing Roger had said Ronna instead of Caroline. Roger explained how he had met with Caroline's spirit guide and how they had come up with a plan together. "She is peaceful now and can move forward in life, in short, she believes your strange story."

"Well, that's wonderful news, isn't it, John?" said Clara, turning to John and holding his hand in hers.

"Yes, it is. I'm happy to hear that, she could never believe me."

"It was her human condition and lack of faith that prevented her from accepting it," said Roger. "I sense, John, that you are not overjoyed at hearing this news, am I mistaken?"

"Yes, what's the matter, John?" asked Clara, noticing his lukewarm reception at Roger's update.

"My concern is not really for Caroline," said John. "I'm glad to hear that she now accepts that I wasn't lying, but my anxiety is for Ronna. How can she move forward? I thought we were working for Ronna."

"We are working for her," said Roger, "things are moving, slowly maybe, but still moving. I just got news before I came here that Peter will no longer have to walk the avenue of atonement. His soul has been freed of its sin and if he gets permission, will be able to send a sign to his sister. So, you see, John, things are moving towards a conclusion."

"That's all very well," said John, "and I'm happy for Peter, but Ronna's unhappy state of mind is due to me being gone from her life. You may leave feathers here and there and Peter can too, but it won't be enough for her. I know Ronna."

"Our work is not yet complete with Ronna," said Roger, "it will come right in the end. Don't you who dwell here have any faith?" John felt embarrassed.

"Yes, of course, I'm sorry, I appreciate the work you are doing."

"Good," said Roger, "I must leave now, but we'll speak again soon." He began to glow and in seconds he disappeared.

"I hope I didn't annoy him," said John, feeling bad. Clara laughed and put her arm around John's shoulders.

"You can't annoy anybody here. You haven't been here long enough to realise that. In time you will learn. Ronna will move forward, just you wait and see."

"Come on," said John, "I feel like a walk in the hills." And they left the porch, hand in hand.

Chapter 49

One day, Ronna was sitting in the office entering invoices on the computer. She'd been working very hard and had not stopped for a lunch break. The day was quite warm, and she had left the office door open to let some air in. She suddenly noticed the smell of burning coal and wondered where it was coming from.

She went outside and looked around the yard but couldn't see any sign of fire anywhere. There was nobody in the yard as the workers had gone to the far field to clear ditches. She walked to the gate and looked up and down the narrow road, but nothing seemed out of place. She turned to walk back towards the office and saw smoke coming from the chimney of John's room.

She rushed across the yard and ran up the steps. Ronna pushed the door open and saw a fire burning in the grate. She knew it couldn't have been any of the workers as they were forbidden to go near the room, and they wouldn't have gone to the trouble of making a fire there. She went in and closed the door behind her. She sat in front of the blaze and waited. Ronna stared into the flames and tried to relax. She remembered how she used to do this when she was a child. A face started to form in the fire, and she soon recognised her brother Peter.

"Peter, oh Peter, it's you. I'm so happy to see you again," and Ronna started to cry.

"Don't cry, Ronna," said Peter in his old familiar voice, "I am well and happy. I couldn't contact you before this time, but now I can. You can now know that I am somewhere and have not vanished into nothingness. I knew a fire would bring us together again. I couldn't send you a sign because of the serious wrong I did in life. I took a lot of money as you know which wasn't mine to take, and I had to atone. I brought shame on my family. All is well here now though and I'm happy."

"Oh Peter," said Ronna, "if you only knew how sad I was after you left my life. The memories of our times together, though pleasant were too painful to think of. I work here now and am in charge. I'm still living at home and drive here to Risk during the week. The rest of the family are all well but miss you terribly. What do you do there?"

"I walk, I read, I learn and I love. It was a beautiful place to come to after being so sick. I have to go now, but I will send you signs from time to time."

"Oh, please don't go yet," pleaded Ronna, "can't you stay a bit longer?" Peter smiled at her. "There's somebody else who wants to talk with you, and I must make way. Stay where you are and keep your eyes on the flames. Goodbye for now Ronna but remember, look out for signs." Peter's face vanished from the fire and Ronna held her gaze. Nothing happened for a minute, and she hoped she wouldn't be disappointed. Suddenly, the room grew cold despite the fire and an odd feeling came over her. One of the flames stretched higher than the others and John's face appeared in it. It was the face he'd worn as Mark Foynes.

"Hello, Ronna," he said, smiling.

"John, it's you, I knew somehow you'd come back. It's too hard for me here without you."

"I felt terrible leaving you that note, but there was no other way. I knew about your sadness, and I wanted to help you. It's only now that I was able to with the help of others here. I met Peter, he's very nice. His mistake in life made it impossible for him to send you a sign. From now on, he will send you feelings of comfort and peace."

"I know he will," said Ronna, "everything is making sense at last."

"This place is the next stage," said John, "you must live out your life on earth first and then come here. I grew blind in my time there and had no light in my eyes, that is until I came back and met you. You gave me the power to live and love again. I was very lucky to get the opportunity of knowing you."

"It's still very sad for me, I can't move forward and am forever looking back. It's making me quite miserable."

"Think of your life now and in the future," said John, "it's all in steps; you are about to move on to the next one."

"I wonder," replied Ronna, sadly.

"We will meet again," said John. This was what Ronna wanted to hear. She had felt that John had vanished from her life without a trace, and that she would never see him again. His words coming from the fire gave her the comfort she so desperately needed.

"Think of how you helped me," said John, "how you gave meaning to a life that had lost it. I plunged into the darkness of death with an empty bitterness in my heart, and you reached out to me. Only a person who knows what true love is would have done so."

"I've been to your grave John, and Clara's. I know about her. Will she be there when we meet again?"

"Yes," he replied, "but it will all be clearer when your time comes. Life here is not the same as on earth. It's hard for the human mind to comprehend. You have not lost me." A feeling of happiness and peace passed through Ronna at these words. She felt the burden of memories lifting from her. She began to see a way forward and how she could move along that way now. "Will you visit me again?" she asked.

"No," replied John, "but take comfort from the fact that we will meet again. Now you must carry on, live your life, and learn to love again, just as I did. I think you'll find someone will reach out to you too. I must go now, but know I am always here and Peter too." The fire started to die down and John said goodbye.

"Goodbye, my love," replied Ronna, and suddenly the fire vanished leaving an empty grate.

Ronna walked out to the steps and felt happiness as she looked at the clouds moving slowly across the sky. She touched the horseshoe above her head as she had seen John doing many times. "Life is for living," she said to herself, "and I will live my life as I should do. I also have the comfort of knowing that life continues beyond this. Not many people can say that." She closed the red door behind her and walked down the stone steps.

From the author that brought you *The Sad Windows*